Sugar Mama

A KEILANII JENNINGS SAGA

"She Who Laughs Last, Laughs Best"

BY

Lalanii Wilson Jones

WITH TREAVION DAVENPORT

ISBN: 978-0-578-65033-3 (Paperback)
Library of Congress Control Number: 2020903436

Front Cover Illustration by Aaron Starkey
Book Design by Rena Violet

Printed by Mcnaughton & Gunn in the United States of America

First Printing Edition 2020.

Mogul 24/7 LLC
8330 LBJ Freeway
Suite 420
Dallas, Texas 75243
www.mogul247.com

@sugarmamabook
www.ultimatesugarmama.com

Dedication

Sugar Mama is dedicated to everyone who has been exploited by someone whom they believed loved them for all the right reasons when in fact their motives were all wrong. As the saying goes, "The struggle is real," but it doesn't have to be. By merely loving yourself and setting clear boundaries, you can stop a user and a loser in their tracks and call them out on their BS! The commitment to loving yourself has to take priority over everything, and always remember, self-preservation is the #1 rule.

My Dearest Ms Starey,
I love you so very
much. You a such a
treasure. You have
impacted my life
in so many ways ♡
I could never thank
you enough

With Love

Jeannie
AKA
Sandy ♡

Contents

Acknowledgments

IT IS MY honor and privilege to thank Treavion Davenport for committing to the *Sugar Mama* project and seeing it through to completion. Cheers to us! Together we invested countless hours of conversation, observation, research, resilience, and frequent-flyer miles during the three years that it took to bring this work to life. No matter the diversions or direction our journey took, you stayed the course. I'm eternally grateful for Treavion aka "Sweet-n-Low" and our spiritual sister, Kayla Tucker Adams. She introduced the two of us and is always positive, progressive and pulling talents and gifts out of me that I did not know I had. I have to thank all of my mentors and tried and true prayer warriors. If you were with me in the pit of my struggles, encouraging me while never passing judgment, then know that I eternally love you and appreciate every conservation, meal, and prayer that you shared on my behalf.

While I cannot name everyone, it's mandatory that I acknowledge the following: Dr. David E. Wilson, my pastor, please know that I meditate on every word you've spoken to me. I appreciate your heartfelt texts and prayers for me and my family. Geraldine Allison, affectionately known as Granny, God made more than enough in a human being when He made you. Our morning pep talks and prayers mean the world to me. You never wavered and stood strong in your convictions and faith that God would see me through. He did! Your words carried me when I could not carry myself, you are irreplaceable. Dr. Thelma B. Brown, my beloved Aunt Thelma, my treasure; your wisdom is infinite. Your timeless advice has never failed. I'm so grateful for the knowledge and optimism you have imparted in my life. To Shirley Brigham, I thank you for taking all of my calls, being an empathetic ear to my concerns and showing me unending love. I also wish to express gratitude to all of my brothers; you know who you are! You carried me during the most trying time of my life. Your presence restored my faith in black men. And to my brother Russell Wilson II, "thank you" doesn't seem sufficient to represent the eternal appreciation and respect I have for the man that you are. "I am my brother's keeper" resonates deeply when it comes to you!

Thank you, God, for the total experience. With your mercy and grace, I endured, I overcame and as a result, was able to give life to *Sugar Mama.* Because of your blessings, her story may be a cautionary tale to others. The saga continues!

~Lalanii Wilson-Jones aka Keilani Jennings aka Sugar

I WISH TO THANK my professional and spiritual sister Kayla Tucker Adams for having the foresight and the cohesive spirit to connect Lalanii and me. I will always honor that and appreciate all of the amazing opportunities that have manifested as a result of the trifecta we have become. I learned a lot about myself and so many others who find themselves the victim of a lover motivated solely by self-serving intentions. Most of all it's my honor to acknowledge the one and only Lalanii Wilson Jones aka "Sugar." I thank the Father for blessing our work together, our friendship and our sisterhood bond. From the moment I met this 5'1" firecracker powerhouse, I have been nothing but blessed, impressed, and better dressed! Thank you, Lanii, for trusting me to help tell this story and share this message of empowerment to countless victims of users, abusers, and those who mistake kindness for weakness. This is only the beginning because, as you know, the saga continues...

~Treavion Davenport aka Sweet-n-Low

Prologue

This petty motherfucker…

TO THINK, AFTER setting my ex-husband up with a monthly payroll check of over $8,000, for which he did absolutely nothing to earn, an actual 401K for the first time in his measly existence, top-tier health insurance, paying his child support, lavishing him and his ungrateful-ass kids with exotic trips, designer clothes, and fine jewelry, investing in one whack business idea and scheme after the other and upgrading him in every fucking, fathomable way, this low down excuse for a man had the unmitigated gall to squabble over a damn Sam's Club card and his 24-Hour Fitness membership as part of our divorce settlement. This petty motherfucker took being petty to the lowest depths imaginable.

Do you know how embarrassing that is, to sit there in court while the man I married reduces himself to demanding that I pay for his discount club shopping card, gym membership, and keep the Amex that I just gave him a month earlier? Who does that?!

You would think that a nigger would want to walk away like a real man, with some dignity and balls intact. But no, not "Petty Wap"; he didn't want to pay for anything. Even the judge knew it was some bullshit and shook his head with disdain as he said,

"Give him the fitness membership and Sam's Club card, Mrs. Jennings, but don't worry, he won't touch the American Express."

Because of Texas law, he was entitled to half of the equity in "our" home, mind you, he never paid one dime for it, but hey that's the law. The mother fucker hadn't lived in the house for six months. Amazing, what a come-up for him. He was also entitled to half of my 401K, so he cleared about $375K on that for all the work I put in. He also got the Chrysler 300 that was wrapped with one of my company's logos on it, I even had to pay the $600 to have the wrap taken off. But Karma is a hot bitch, and that damn car doesn't even work now, and he can't afford to repair it.

It's crazy to me how he expected to be able to live the same lifestyle he lived with me but never lifted a finger to help me do shit. For some reason he expected me to continue to pay for his baller lifestyle, while he plotted with an incompetent lawyer bitch to blindside me with a "complex divorce" using the proceeds of the unauthorized sale of one of my BMWs! But what's for me is for me and not much gets past Sugar Mama. I will live to thwart his plans, and he will live to hate the day he tried to play me.

"Sugar is for the body as narcissism is for the soul. Both pleasures kill."

—Robin Sacredfire, *Mystic Poet and Novelist*

ONE

Let's Not Sugar Coat It

EVEN THOUGH HE was right up under my nose for over a decade, it really didn't become apparent to me how treacherous Elliot Jr. really was until I stumbled on an unassuming envelope that was never intended for my eyes. The fateful correspondence, however, contained a receipt for the retainer he had just paid to file for a complex divorce. I knew we had some issues in our marriage, and that he had wielded a ridiculous ultimatum regarding me making my son, Sozey, "bow down" to him following a brawl at my office. But really, had it gotten that deep or complex? Without so much as one word, hint, or discussion and in spite of all that I had done for that bastard and his demon spawn, everything had boiled down to that very moment, and it was on. Sugar

Mama was about to make it real simple for this nigger who turned out to be a bona fide gold digger.

Once the shit hit the fan, he must have been sick because his lifestyle changed drastically. It tickles me just to think about it because, in the blink of an eye, this digger went from having a decadent roof over his head in one of Dallas' most posh neighborhoods to living out of his third-rate upholstery shop workspace, zoned in an industrial area. The last I heard, Elliot Jr. was getting good use of his 24-Hour Fitness membership to shower and change and had become well known at the Ace America Pawn Shop, where he hocked everything with any value. As the saying goes, "She who laughs last, laughs best," he he, motherfucker!

It was nothing but God's grace that spared me from falling victim to his plan to take me for half or even more of my fortune. I think he was probably trying to get all his ducks in a row, liquidate or hide the assets that I worked hard for, or worse, steal from me, but his ass got exposed just in time. Had we remained married for at least ten years, Elliot Jr. could have been rightfully entitled to alimony and a huge chunk of my paper and multiple businesses that he never lifted a finger to build. February 14, 2019, would have marked the 10-year threshold; instead, our complex divorce was finalized on November 3, 2017.

Before we get into all of the gory details of the legal dissolution of our so-called marriage, let's rewind a bit and get into how I hooked up with this loser in the first place.

I have known Elliot Jr. since my daughter, Suga Baby, was 3 months old; she was born in April of 2000. Her father had been gunned down during my pregnancy and I had felt so alone. I met him in August of that same year. I don't think I ever actually fell in love with him, I just liked him a lot plus he was easy on the eyes. By the time we were married, I was about to turn 40 and although I had already made a damn good life for myself, my son Sozey, and princess Suga Baby, I was ready to build an empire with someone.

I actually met Elliot Jr. over the telephone. I called my friend Jackie at her home and instead, he answered the phone. I didn't know who he was or anything, but I didn't like the way he came off as arrogant and rude, so I just demanded, "Put Jackie on the phone." He said, "That's not how you call somebody's house and ask to speak to them." I came back at him like, "Well, that's not how you answer somebody's phone!" or something to that effect. So, we got into an argument until Jackie took the phone and I asked her, "Who was that clown?" She was like, "Oh girl, don't pay him no mind, that's just Elliot Jr., Sonny's cousin". She was laughing at us and one thing led to another but before our conversation was over, Jackie said, "Girl, Elliot Jr. asked can he call you?" I was like, "Not talking like that. He doesn't know how to answer the phone." She said, "Aw Sugar. don't be like that, I'm gonna put him on the phone." So, the next thing I heard was "Someone this spicy, gotta be sweet...I need to see you."

A few days later he came over. I can't lie, I was anxious to see who was making all this noise on the phone. I peeped out the window and saw a '92 Buick Glass House and wondered who still drove those. When I opened the door and looked up at his 6-foot frame, I was like, "Okay, I can work with this." He was very good looking with a caramel-colored complexion, a redbone with a nice smile. His arms seemed either too long or too short for his frame, I could never decide, but I instantly had the thought that his arms were too short to box with God. I kept that to myself, though.

We were both open-minded about relationships, not too pressed for a commitment right away. Honestly, I sensed that he just wanted to have fun, relax, and chill. That wasn't a problem for me because I was still coping with the tragic and sudden loss of Suga Baby's father, so although I longed for the companionship, I wasn't interested in being tied down. You know, I was just open to having a good time and not being in the cuffed zone. I had a house over in the Pleasant Grove area, so our first date was at a nearby IHOP. I had my baby girl with me in her little carrier and in standard fashion, we were both dressed to the nines. When he greeted me, he immediately took the carrier out of my hands and opened the door for me. I remember us being at the restaurant and the waitress saying, "Oh, she looks just like her daddy." So, I looked toward him then we locked eyes, then he raised his eyebrow and we both just burst out laughing. The waitress looked all confused but neither of us offered any explanation, we just made light of the moment, it was funny. That was the thing that I liked most about Elliot Jr., we could easily have a good time.

He and his eldest daughter's mother had recently lost a newborn baby girl who died in the hospital, so Elliot Jr. and I talked about our experiences and, I guess, we developed a significant level of compassion for the other. We knew some people in common, enjoyed the same music and a love for the Dallas Cowboys so an unexpected bond formed between us.

We started dating and seeing each other, I only went to his house a few times, though. He had a roommate in an apartment and Sugar doesn't go to other people's houses like that. Even back then I didn't, I'm not the girl that's gonna come hang out at your house. Typically, there has to be something going on or we'd be en route to doing something, but just to hang out at your bachelor pad, naw, that's not me. You can come to kick it at my house because, admittedly, I'm a bit particular, I have a high taste level and am very cognizant of my surroundings. He was cool with that, so we rolled with it.

During the initial stages of our relationship, I was seeing other people. I'm assuming he dated as well, we were very off and on, off and on, off and on for a nice little while. I can truly say that it was handled with discretion and respect on both ends because there were never any issues or incidents that caused me to think otherwise. To keep it all the way real, I maintained an all-star team of guys whom I dated up until we got married because, prior to that, it wasn't like my relationship with Elliot Jr. was a for sure thing. What man is really? He did little sideways shit that made me raise an eyebrow or take notice here and there, like stumble over his words when I ask where he'd been, but he wasn't a dog the whole time. He was totally different back then and he thought highly of me. However, to hear him tell it during our divorce, I "enslaved him". That's right, he had the audacity to accuse me of enslaving him, like *he* was the victim. I was so embarrassed when I heard him say, "She knew what time it was, she paid me to sleep with her... After a while, it was like I was her love slave." He also proclaimed to be this big gigolo; so what slave gets paid? That wasn't all, according to Elliot Jr., I was physically, verbally, and emotionally abusive to him. There was even a time at the beginning of the marriage when he called the police on me. Even in a sexy, 5"1' package, my bark is ferocious, and my bite is deadly. The situation escalated to a level that law enforcement had to be called. But I'll tell you, Elliot Jr. had done the majority of the barking and biting. Come to think of it, he was always a bit on the dramatic side. That particular incident got heated because I knew he was up to some slick shit with a sneaky bitch and I wasn't having it. I caught the tail end of a conversation when I came into the theater room of our home, which sounded a little too friendly. When he realized I was standing in the doorway he damn near jumped out of his seat, and abruptly ended the call.

Prior to all the drama, for the most part, Elliot Jr. was charming, comical and kept me laughing, I think that's what I liked about him the beginning. Shit, ultimately it had to be his personality because he didn't have anything else to offer. He had no education, notable talent, and unreliable testosterone levels. Heaven knows he didn't have any money! I used to get a kick out of all of his antics and attempts to get paid; in fact, his life was a joke, and he kept me amused until I found myself cutting the check for his next big idea. He had tried to do a multitude of things, but nothing seemed to work out for him and that was okay for a while because as my momma used to say, "Nothing beats a failure but a try". I'd listen to all of his schemes and dreams and I sincerely wanted him to succeed, so I supported a lot of the madness for a very long time. But when you dissect it, he literally didn't have anything coming into the relationship, so why did I think that suddenly with my money and resources on the line that he was going to make it work?

After dealing with him for a while, I came to grips with the fact that Elliot Jr. was not a good provider, but the companionship was great. His tongue knew how to work its way around a uterus but that was about the extent of his intimacy assets. The sex wasn't mind-blowing, nor was it all that frequent. Hell, we weren't married yet, so when he was unavailable, I never missed a beat. I was still sleeping with other people; shit I loved sex and I'm really good at it. That's right, I'm a tried and true freak in the sheets, but I've never been emotionally tied to sex whatsoever. Believe me, when I'm in it, I'm trying to win it. I'm not gonna stalk you or call you, but I am going to blow your mind with the lengths I go to, to ensure I achieve pleasure in the bedroom. When brothers get a pass to Sugarland, they get sprung. I always get the callbacks and questions like "Why haven't I heard from you?" or "Is everything okay?" I'm like, "Yeah nigga, everything is good! I'm working. I will call you when I get a chance." They never know what to do with themselves at that point.

I think that's what happened in Elliot Jr.'s case, he had a sweet tooth when it came to our sex, but as I said, he was alright, and he wasn't consistent enough for me. I was more turned on by his innate sense of humor, wittiness and deep voice. That was sufficient for me until it wasn't. Like I said, at first he was easy on the eyes, nice smooth skin and color like an Indian, but over time he had smoked so much weed and Lord only knows what else, that his skin looked ashen, his teeth were turning yellow, his breath lingered of the scent of pussy and he just wasn't as attractive anymore.

I suppose I was attractive to him, he used to give me compliments and whatnot, but for me personally, I've never relied on compliments or sought approval from a man. See, I'm a mogul in the making, I got a lot going on and I don't need or thrive on the accolades of a man to validate me. So, I'm sure Elliot Jr. said those kinds of things, but for the most part, it fell on deaf ears. A lot of times he would tell me that I was not hearing what he was saying. He expressed that he felt very much like his voice was in the background throughout our on-again, off-again relationship. I'm sure he was right. The truth is there were things that he did, or better yet didn't do, that completely turned me off. I'm the type that, if I am turned off, that's it, the switch has been deactivated. It would damn near take an act of Congress or God to get me back to that place. But Elliot Jr. and I had some history, for the most part, we clicked and there would be periods when he would try to turn me on again, so every so often I would give him another shot.

I think I even surprised myself when I gave him a shot at the actual crown. We were in Las Vegas when we decided to get married. There's not a lot to tell, something came over me. We woke up in our suite, went over to the courthouse to get a marriage license and from there we went to the Little White Wedding Chapel and made an appointment. It was close to midnight before they could get us in, so we made arrangements and planned to come back that evening. I knew that if I chose to do it back home in Dallas, it would have been a big affair and a bunch of rigamarole among the families and whatnot, so we agreed to just keep it low key. So, I didn't get a traditional wedding dress or anything, I had a purple dress in my suitcase that I wore, and he had some jeans or slacks and a blazer. We dressed simply, but tasteful—no matter what, I always step out in style.

Nobody gets married to get divorced unless they have an ulterior motive in mind. I had good intentions and as much as I hate to admit it now, I was hopeful. I guess "happily ever after" just wasn't in our deck of cards and I'm good with that, now. But I'd be lying if I said it didn't take me a while to accept it.

It didn't work, we didn't work, I get it. My thing is, damn don't try to take me to the cleaners to maintain your status and the lifestyle and that I created for us, especially when you know that you didn't contribute anything. Yet somehow you think you're entitled? Naw, bruh!

Sometimes I wish I could just get in his brain, take a deep look into his psyche to get a real understanding of what compelled him to flip the script and where this sense of entitlement came from. To some large degree I take responsibility for spoiling this nigga, I mean I AM SUGAR MAMA. Thanks to my generosity, he acquired quite a few nice things over the years; clothes, jewelry, cars, lavish trips, and hardcore cash. But to be honest, I stopped buying him stuff like that a few years back due to his lack of gratitude.

Gratitude goes a long way with me. It's just one of those things, you don't have to kiss my ass, but you have to be thankful and show some form of appreciation even if it's just a simple "thank you" versus acting like you just got it like that.

After a while it was like all I heard was "You didn't give me this or you didn't do that", then it was "I need this, you know I need that". It got so bad that when I would buy his ass an outfit or shoes to make sure he looks decent when we go somewhere or just a gift and he'd say, "I'd rather have the money." That's so tacky, I hated that. To me, that means that you don't want shit from me but my money, thank you for letting me know. His gimmie, gimmie tantrums about money started to turn my stomach and after a while, there was no turning back.

I guess I could have been more subservient to him. I know that's what he wanted. In fact, those were his words. "The man is the leader of the household, it doesn't matter who makes the most money". So, I guess I was supposed to let him lead the household, but he couldn't keep up with his own child support payments, let alone hold down a job or balance a checkbook. To me, that was some bullshit.

I paid all the bills, brought all the food, kept a nice roof over our heads, made sure that we were riding in style with a multitude of options and financed our lives with all the bells and whistles. So how was he supposed to be the head of the household and control the money that he never earned? Trust me, if Elliot Jr. actually knew how much money I made, he would have driven himself crazy trying to get a hold of it or dictate how it was spent. He knew that my income was high, but he had no idea how much I was generating, what my companies were bringing in and all the investments I had that were earning money while I slept. He could see a lot of cash flow, but he didn't necessarily know where it was coming from, and that drove him crazy. Instead of just being a helpmate, or living in comfort and peace, he had to be an ass.

Things between us started to get progressively worse when he began insisting that we join the church of his choice and then tithe. Now if he was really that man, I mean one whose choices I could respect and look to for real, grounded direction, then I might have seriously considered it. But not only had I attended my church home, Dallas First Baptist, since before Suga Baby was born, but Elliot Jr. didn't even know those folks. He only chose that church because some people he was trying to impress attended service there and he wanted to floss. He was good for trying to front for and stunt on people; but not at my expense. I wasn't feeling that. I guess I was supposed to just stop worshipping at my beloved church. Boy, bye. There was something about the whole thing that felt shady to me; he kept going on and on about being the head of the household, but it fell deaf ears.

I thought the subject was dead completely until a month or so later when I ran into this real gossipy chick named Carla at the hair salon and she hit me with "Hey girl, I didn't know y'all had joined my church." I must have looked confused because she quickly offered, "Yeah, I saw your husband's picture on the 'New Member' board and I was wondering where your picture was." I just laughed and was like, "Girl, you can keep on looking," and proceeded to change the subject. When I saw Elliot Jr. later, I just shook my head and laughed. That happened a lot 'cause he was so simple, stupid and would lie over the pettiest shit. I learned to laugh to keep from crying or cutting him.

Now, don't get me wrong, even though a Sugar Mama pays the cost to be the boss if Elliot Jr. had shown himself to be a helpmate, a partner or better yet a real man outside of the bedroom, then I would have been more open or flexible about how we handled our finances.

Let me break it down for you. For starters, I put my husband on a $100,000-plus salary; most people would have been satisfied with that, but he wasn't. I mean he was given over $8,000 a month, yet he didn't pay one bill and would still complain, "Keilanii, I don't have money for this," or "I still need money for that..." or "This ain't enough money." If he had worked and added to his income, then he could have made it be enough, but not this digger, you see what I'm saying?

Every now and again, he would get an odd job, but he never held it down for long, and Lord knows he never held me down. Instead, he relied on me, and I can't even blame him completely because Sugar Mama enabled him to do a lot of things that he would not have been able to do. Had I just insisted that he work, contribute or be accountable for something, maybe things would have turned out differently. Maybe they would have turned out worse; I might have had to lower my standards and lessen the quality of my lifestyle. Then again, if I would have had to meet him at his hand, ain't no telling how I would have been living; instead of dining at Eddie V's, we would have been eating at Mickey D's.

Still, I don't see what his problem was; like I said, from the salary he received from me, he took home somewhere around $4,000 dollars every two weeks before deductions. He was already behind in his child support, and once his jealous ass baby mommas found out I was in the picture, honey, they had the Texas Attorney General on his head. I was married to him, so I had his back and wanted to do the right thing, so I set it up so that the support payments came directly out of those checks. What he did with his little twos and fews after that was on him, that was his play money. I didn't really know what he was doing, and I really didn't care. As far as I was concerned, it was "Negro, don't bother me about haircut money," because he did not pay a single household bill. He wasn't buying me gifts, he never got Suga Baby or Sozey shit of value, nor was he paying for anything for his kids when they came around or otherwise.

I just believe that when a woman has to bear the financial brunt of the relationship or overcompensate for a man's fiscal shortcomings, it affects other aspects of their relationship unless there's a clear cut understanding, lots of love, communication, and respect, with no hidden agendas. Even though I was papered up enough to carry ten times my own weight, I hadn't signed up to be a cash cow for this nigga. Once we broached the idea of marriage, I genuinely entered that union with all the intentions and desires of giving it a go.

I don't know about the next woman, but for me, it grew increasingly hard to be in love with somebody I had to take care of as if he were my child. I didn't give birth to this grown-ass man, hell I had kids, you know what I mean? I like to indulge in the finer things in life and I'm attracted to a man who enjoys and provides the same.

The reality of Elliot Jr. never being a provider became soberly clear to me once we got back from Vegas and the honeymoon was over (no pun intended.) I remember so vividly the day that I laid out all the bills, well, more specifically, the household bills. I set them on the table so he could see everything clearly and get a realistic idea of what the basic household expenses and obligations were. He looked up at me as if he'd seen a ghost and said nothing, so I said, "Pick a bill, baby." I guess that must have tickled him because he literally laughed in my face. I was like "Come on, babe, I got the mortgages, cars and credit cards, you can just pick a bill or two that you want to be responsible for."

Elliot Jr. just stood there, and he boldly said, "Woman, you trippin'! I ain't been paying yo bills and I'm not about to start." At that point, I was trying to figure out if he was being serious. I reasoned with myself that maybe there would just be a little transition period. He was accustomed to living on his own in a small space, so maybe my big house and all the bills that came along with it were overwhelming, so I tried to be patient.

It had been about two months and I noticed he didn't offer to pay for anything. He had moved in all his clothes, belongings, had parked his raggedly little car and started rocking whips from my fleet. No exaggeration, if you were to look up the word "upgrade" in the dictionary, I swear my photo would be right there.

Elliot Jr. is a poor excuse for a man. He never kicked in, not even once. Not when he worked, half-ass hustled and worse, not even when I put him on the payroll for doing absolutely nothing. He smoked a lot of weed, blew money at the strip clubs, and let me not fail to mention his little recreational coke usage. I found out about that little nugget when he was deemed uninsurable by my life insurance provider following a drug test. Elliot Jr. was notorious for this type of fuckery. Why even go so far as to take a drug test when you know you are going to drop dirty?

When I confronted him about it, he got all defensive and swore that he had just used it one time, like at some random party shit. He was a lying ass nigga, 'cause two years later, when I had him tested for the life insurance policy again, he failed. We had to wait a minimum of 18 months to even apply again, and like deja vu, his low-life ass embarrassed me. My insurance agent just dropped her head and looked down at her paperwork and said, "I'm sorry, Mrs. Jennings, for the same reason as before, I am unable to issue a policy for Mr. Jennings at this time."

When I look back on it, I don't think he cared about anybody but himself and for the most part his two daughters. The second life insurance mishap happened sometime in 2012 or 2013; after that, we went through a period when I became so frustrated with his bullshit and separated. Shortly after, I went through a stressful season for my businesses and I let my guard down. He acted like he was so concerned, I guess I was just feeling a little vulnerable and not long after we got back together. The thing is when I take vows or give my word to do something, I use everything in my power to keep my end of the bargain. I mean Elliot Jr. didn't have a pot to piss in when I met him, so his piss poor finances weren't going to be the reason I severed the marriage. I didn't marry him for money, I always relied on myself for financial sustenance, so where his behaviors regarding finances might have turned the average woman off immediately, my tolerance must have been a little higher. Although Elliot Jr. wasn't exactly what you might describe as passionate or affectionate, there were times that he would be sweet. He would pick up my favorite ice cream, and bring home candy or toys for the kids. He was the only man that Suga Baby had ever been around, so at some point, we decided that as man and wife we were trying to make it work.

But the truth is we really should've gone our separate ways long ago.

So, life went on with me as this nigger's sugar mama and him as my live-in dick, I guess. We always slept in the same bed and he would cuddle with me and from time to time I would allow myself to think that he actually gave a fuck. In hindsight, I realize that he was just playing the role to get more out of his meal ticket.

When it came to handling his own business or seeing things through, he seemed to fail miserably, but when it came to milking my money bag, he excelled at it. He always seemed to show up for big-ticket purchase days like when I would add to my fleet or VIP outings like using my season tickets and suite at the Dallas Cowboys and Mavericks games or shopping sprees and travel.

If I hadn't initiated that we spend time together, he never would have. Elliot Jr. had a life of his own and he was entrenched in his motorcycle world. I have a pretty good idea of what goes on at the late-night parties, on these long weekend trips when they would ride out and with the whole biker-hoe culture, but I wasn't really studding him, especially after I knew he used coke and he stopped traveling with me.

I'll never forget our last trip together. We went down to South Beach Miami with three other couples, my close girlfriends and their men. For two days straight, we all dined, luxuriated by the pool, and balled out at Bal Harbour Shops where trust-fund babies and gold-diggers with impeccable taste shop till they drop.

Once we got back to the room I crashed. Elliot Jr. slipped out of the bed, took a shower, got dressed in his new shit and hit the streets. When it was time to meet the other couples for dinner and drinks, this nigger was Missing in Action. Me and a couple of the guys blew his phone up, calling and texting back to back. A few of our friends were worried about his ass, but I was pissed beyond pisstivity and worse, I was embarrassed. I pasted on the best-unbothered smile on my face, threw back a few top-shelf lemon drop martinis with sugared rims, posed for some selfies and partied with my peeps until about 3 am. About an hour or so later, Elliot Jr.'s trifling ass slithers in wreaking of whiskey while I was in the shower. When I got out, I acted like he didn't exist because to me at that point he did not. I packed the rest of my things and we headed to the lobby for our car to take us to the airport for our 6 am flight back to Dallas. He tried to plead his case and lay his head on my shoulder to soothe his headache but I wasn't interested.

Several days passed before I uttered a single word to him. No matter how I tried, what I did for his ass, or how many times I forgave him, tried to rise above and press reset, Elliot Jr. always managed to drain my energy. He had come dangerously close to robbing me of my joy. The only saving grace for this sorry motherfucker was the fact that he had a pretty good relationship with my hearts: Suga Baby and Sozey.

I couldn't imagine the depths of larceny and betrayal that Elliot Jr. would resort to in punishing me for closing the bank on his petty ass. He knew that nothing and no one mattered more to me than my children, so when he made the fateful mistake of going there, there was no turning back. Nobody fucks with my sugar babies and gets away with it…

"Images are deceiving. Salt and sugar look exactly the same but taste very different."

—Suzy Kassem, *Rise Up and Salute the Sun: The Writings of Suzy Kassem*

TWO

When The Shit Hits The Fan

WHEN ELLIOT JR. and I got married, his girls were probably about four or five, somewhere in there. He was very behind in his child support payments, but he loved his daughters. He would attempt to comb their hair, teach them to tie their shoelaces and made sure they knew that even though they didn't live together that he was only a phone call away. I never had that kind of bond with my father, so that kind of warmed my heart. I had no problem with him having a strong relationship with his children because I've always made my children a top priority. Some people might describe how I take care of my kids as "spoiling" them, but to me, I just approach everything on a higher level. There's no way I'm going to be sporting Gucci,

Versace, Giuseppe, and Louis Vuitton and my kids wear Walmart clothes. That's not to offend or judge parents who do shop there and dress their families in bargain brands, but the reality for me is, I don't dress like that so why should Suga Baby and Sozey dress like that?

My thing is if I can afford it and we ain't missing a beat over here, then what we do and how we do it is on me. The problem came after a while when Elliot Jr. started expecting me to buy and do for his kids the way I did for mine. I mean he literally felt like I should be buying his girls high-priced, designer clothes and neither he nor their mommas ever dressed them like that. One of the girl's mamas was a manager at Didi's Discount and another of his baby mommas loved JCPenney. I mean she swore they were doing it like they had just stepped out of Neiman Marcus. I'm not trying to make a joke about the kids at all or parents who can't or who choose not to spend a lot of money on clothes, I'm just saying it got to the point where he expected me to upgrade him and his kids and do things for them that he nor their mommas were doing. At first, it was cool; when I bought for mine, I bought for his, I'm just wired like that. Plus, I'm the type that likes to step out a certain way. So, I'm not going to have Suga Baby poppin' and shining and his children rolling with me looking like misfits. I looked at it like, they would have something to wear nice when they stayed at our house, which they did so on the regular, so the clothes and shoes I purchased would be used for our outings. It only became an issue when Elliot Jr. started letting them take all of their stuff home and somehow when they would come back, they never seemed to bring back the nice things I had got them. So, I would have to go buy more and the cycle would continue. It got to the point where he wanted me to buy them two sets of clothes, and I wasn't going to do all that. Eventually, he would just come right out and say, "Why can't they live the same lifestyle we live?" That was a light bulb moment for me, I realized that he was not only delusional but that I had created a monster. And this went on for a long while. It became clear to me that he was rotten, and as they say, the fruit don't fall far from the tree. As I spoiled him, this evolved into a sense of entitlement and to be honest he also developed a sense of resentment toward me and my kids, but I didn't know it at the time. As much as I am a businesswoman and mogul in the making, I'm very much a family person. I love to cook and believe me Sugar Mama can burn. I love to have a nice, comfortable home and ride in style. I enjoy the lavish things in life, and I revel in the opportunity to travel. This was no exception when I was with Elliot Jr. and therefore, he and his offspring reaped the benefits of my zest for life. So, it wasn't like Suga Baby got all the bells and whistles and they got nothing, hell naw! I don't even roll like that. We went on family outings, out to fine restaurants, excursions, and 5-star vacations. I remember the time I paid for all of us to go on a trip to Hawaii. This was literally the Hawaiian experience you see in the brochures, from the high-end resort to the luau, hula show, black sand beaches, and decadent dining. The fate of the trip was already challenged when I discovered that his kids' mommas clearly didn't know how to pack a bag for a tropical getaway. I mean there were no flip flops, changes of swimsuits, visors, sunscreen, or really any decent matching short sets or sundresses. I was stuck between being baffled and mortified. All I could do is shake my head, but it was too late and complaining wasn't going to solve anything, so I ended up spending double, if not more buying things in Hawaii for the children to function.

The part that tripped me out and really got under my skin was their lack of gratitude. Elliot Jr. had gotten so bad with it that he had convinced himself that he deserved or was entitled to all of this. In hindsight, it was as if he saw me as a limitless ATM, that he never had to service or replenish. Sadly, he passed these bad attributes on to his bay bays because they had become notorious for not saying thank you or showing any form of appreciation. Moreover, they too started growing more brazen with their demands and expectations.

On one of the last days in Hawaii, the five of us (me, Elliot Jr., his two kids, and Suga Baby) went on an excursion called the "Road to Hana," where you experience the most gorgeous black and red sand beaches, walking trails and waterfalls. For lunch, we decided on a nice local restaurant with an incredible view. As a fine diner myself, for the most part, I had no qualms with the kids exploring the menu or even trying new things, but when his 10-year-old insisted on ordering a $50 steak at lunch, I had to speak up about that. Now for the rest of the whole trip, we couldn't get her to try anything except for a chicken Caesar salad, but for some reason, for this meal, she was dead set on ordering a highly-priced hunk of beef in the early afternoon. Elliot Jr. never had my back when it came to shit like this; on the contrary, he insisted that I was antagonizing her. He told me to chill and to stop complaining like it wasn't such a big deal and that he wasn't about to limit his kids to ordering from the kiddie menu. Don't get me wrong, I wanted them to have a memorable vacation experience, but I found this behavior alarming. In the end, I chose to be petty on the inside and bask in the pleasure of watching her struggle to eat every bite of the steak. I'm all for children, and adults for that matter, trying different things, but that's only cool if the experimentation is on your dime. From day one it was on me and at that point, I realized that the monster I had created had spawned two mini monsters right before my very eyes. Rather than have an argument about it, I hatched a plan to get their glutenous asses, that's how "Hot Dog Night" was born. The next time it was their week to visit, I pulled out my trusty crockpot, boiled a couple of packs of beef franks, and set out a generous spread of toppings. I do everything on a certain level, so it was still nice, but most certainly, "Hot Dog Night" was invented as a result of their overindulgence.

I wasn't the only one who began to change and pull back, Elliot Jr. had started that behavior long before I even tapped into how bad things had gotten. For the longest time, he and Suga Baby were pretty close. She was an infant we met, and he was well aware that her father was deceased. I believed that he had taken a genuine interest in her. Other than her uncles and her big brother Sozey, who was 7 when she was born, Elliot Jr. was the only man in her life. He always asked about her, went with us on outings, and they did things together. But over the course of time, while I built my businesses, and added to my fortune, he added to his family and had three children with three different women; a son who lived with his mother in another state and two little girls, both the same age who lived equal distance on the other side of town. When he and I did get more involved, and things got more serious, he and my daughter got tighter as well. We did things together and really enjoyed our little family unit. Over the years I guess he started to feel bad that he wasn't involved in his own children's lives as he was with Suga Baby. He had been completely cut off from his son, and I think he felt guilty for slacking as a father and blamed himself for his daughters being socially awkward, extremely introverted and their obvious weirdness. Despite him seeing how dedicated I am to exposing my kids to a variety of things and expanding their horizons, he didn't make any effort to introduce his children to culture or spend time with them outside of every other weekend when they came to stay with us as ordered by the courts. His excuse was that they lived on the other side of town. As our children got older, the differences between them and Suga Baby grew more and more obvious and the tension between our girls was so thick that you could almost taste it. I felt some kind of annoyed by it because I knew that it didn't have anything to do with me or my daughter per se. Elliot Jr. 's girls' issues were manufactured of their own insecurities and jealousy. They were always somewhat disconnected and odd, even when I would have Suga Baby take them to the movies with her or we'd do outings with just the girls they seemed to be void of emotion and never happy, but it didn't stop there. I started noticing some disturbing behaviors in Elliot Jr. toward Suga Baby that got progressively worse; he would yell and curse at her and would be quick to show his irritation with her right in front of his girls. Oh yeah, he was quite the character; when they were around he'd show his ass and act like their shit don't stink, and when they went home, he would suddenly be nicer to my daughter, and try to make her laugh, and make small talk like he used to. Elliot Jr.'s bullshit became more obvious as she got older and like her mama, Suga Baby ain't nobody's fool. Not only did she begin to identify his two-faced antics, but she also called him out on it. It got to the point where she wouldn't go places with him and didn't want to do anything with him. He would still go with us to Suga Baby's cheer competitions, and for the most part, he seemed happy when her team did well, but Dallas cheerleading competitions are high energy, so it's hard to be in a sour mood at one of them, but she knew his interest was fake and she wasn't buying it. Eventually, she withdrew and didn't fool with him at all, but I don't think neither she nor I could ever imagine how spiteful he could be toward her, even if his goal was to hurt me.

Things really got fucked up a couple of years before Suga Baby's epic Sweet 16 affair. One evening she and I came in from a day of shopping and just as I had taken off my bra and was settling into my bed, I heard her yell out, "Mama!" Elliot Jr. wasn't home; he had left out to take his girls home before we got in. I was really startled by the sound of her voice and I knew something wasn't right, so I was ready for some smoke. I grabbed one of my pieces and ran into her room. She was in her closet just screaming with tears running down her face. "Why, Mama? Why?!" It took a second for my eyes to adjust and focus in on what I was seeing, but it took no time for my nose to know that it smelled like shit. Like some actual shit. My poor baby was going nuts because feces was smeared all over her shoes; now you know ladies don't play about their shoes. What kind of animal does that?! When we really assessed the situation, we discovered that there was dog shit smeared, thrown and smashed in her closets. Feces had been smashed all over her shoes, on her hanging clothes, in her drawers, on her walls, and light fixtures. It was like a scene out of a horror movie, I couldn't believe my eyes or my nose for that matter. Come to find out, Elliot Jr. 's demon spawn had desecrated Suga Baby's room and belongings and gave her their asses to kiss. I wish I could tell you that someone had a good explanation, or that his baby mommas called to apologize on their child's behalf or made them reach out to Suga Baby, or that my so-called husband had my back in any way, but that would be too much like right. When they came over during their next visitation weekend, I insisted on a family meeting to address the shitty elephant in the room. I was hoping that Elliot Jr. would show some support as a parent, or at least as a stepparent based on simply doing the right thing, but I couldn't have been more wrong.

They just stayed in their bedroom and showed no real remorse, they were just looking all crazy. They had this blank look; they would just stare not saying anything. But this was nothing new; many times people would greet or speak to them and they wouldn't say anything. I hate that shit; my kids were raised with proper etiquette and respect for others. They were trained; when you walk into a room, you speak and acknowledge other people's presence. Even when I met them at age three, Elliot Jr.'s kids were never warm. In spite of all of the love we had shown them and the experiences my generosity afforded them, they were still resentful toward me and apparently my Suga Baby too. One time he had the nerve to tell me that one of his raggedy-ass baby mammas asked him why their kids couldn't have the same lifestyle that we did and that he agreed with her. I had to tell him, "The lifestyle I created is for me and mine, not for them. First of all, *we* don't work for this lifestyle, I work for it! As for your baby momma with all her opinions, she'll never have what I have because she can never do what I do!" He couldn't say shit, but when I questioned his girls about what they did to Suga Baby's room and explained how bad they made her feel, Elliot Jr. raised up on me and told me to "Shut the fuck up!" He said, "Okay, damn, that's enough, they heard you!" I couldn't believe it, but I knew then that any and all support, provision or consideration for his daughters on my behalf would cease. As for my daughter, she continued to flourish, I replaced her shoes and redecorated her bedroom, their hate resulted in a major upgrade for my baby.

The next few years were a blur; I had grown my childcare empire and had opened a home health care practice which was booming. I knew things between Elliot Jr. and me had been strained but I still had him on the payroll, made sure he stayed up to date with his child support payments and even purchased a new home in one of Dallas's most affluent neighborhoods. See I'm not the average chick, I don't get all caught up in my emotions or strung out on some good dick. One negro could never stop my show, and his bullshit really just backfired on him and drove me to achieve even more success and to enjoy the fruits of my labors. I've always known that I was the prize, and I had raised my baby girl to know this as well. As her sixteenth birthday approached, the anticipation for her big day was palpable. Everyone was so excited and looking forward to the festivities, everyone except Elliot Jr. that is. It wasn't until the actual party was underway that he began to process just how grandly I had set it out for my princess. It was actually comical watching him try to calculate my event budget in his head. I could just see the price tags and estimations calculating in his pea-sized brain. He knew that I normally go all out and that something was being planned. There was Suga Baby's 5-look photoshoot, lots of phone calls with vendors and guests, and of course we shopped for the perfect "Sweet 16" outfits, but he was clueless to the magnitude of her special day. About a week before the party, he asked me if I had invited his daughters and I said something like "Well, I knew that her party is not on a weekend that you are going to have them and I know you aren't going to pick them up and buy them something to wear for this." He was fuming, but he left it at that, and trust and believe that I had no words or feelings about them not being invited.

That night of the party he rode in the limo with us, feasted on the gourmet spread, tried to drown his envy with liquor and jumped all in our photos like he was really doing something, but on the inside he was sick. You could just sense his anger due to all the lavishness. He resented that I had spent so much money on my daughter but didn't spend like that on his kids or him anymore. The icing on the cake was my extra special gift of a customized 2016 Ford Mustang Convertible laced with her favorite color in a bright purple stripe, interior and rims. He could have been sold for a nickel, but that negro wasn't worth a penny and less than a year later he proved just how much he truly loathed me and envied Suga Baby.

"Her words depressed him. They were like spilled sugar; however much you swept it up some grains would keep grinding under your feet."

—Muriel Spark, *Memento Mori*

THREE

God Bless The Child Who Has His Own

I DEFINITELY OVER INDULGED my kids and truth be told, it has backfired in my face. Hindsight being 20/20 I just didn't want them to have to work as hard as I did. From an early age, I had to fend for myself. My mother, Honey made no secret about the fact that I had to get out and get it on my own. "God bless the child who has his own" was her go-to phrase. She constantly instilled in me that if you want something, you gotta work for it. I can't remember a time when Honey just offered me some money or a car or anything for that matter. There was never an occasion where she offered any real encouragement or anything tangible to set me up to go and make something happen for myself. You better believe, if she gave me any money, I had to earn it.

My mother was a very bright and beautiful woman, she valued education and was a registered nurse. I'd have to describe her as an opportunist when it came to men though. She was a trip, to say the least, she married and divorced six times and made no apologies about it. When the thrill was gone or she felt that the well had run dry she had no problem with canceling the check and moving on.

As a little girl, I lived in Germany with my mother and father. My baby brother Randolph Jennings II was actually born there. Our parents met and were married in South Carolina, but my daddy was stationed in the military over there. Honey was a well-trained nurse and easily found work. She had even brought herself a shiny brand spanking new Volkswagen. Things were going pretty good until rumors started to surface about my dad fooling around with some woman on the base. It wasn't long before my mother grew bored and resentful, then decided to retaliate. I was still very young but I remember them arguing quite a lot. One time they were driving through Europe and Honey tried to take the wheel, forcing my father to nearly lose control. She was hysterical and threatening to drive them both off the cliff. It just was a bad relationship. Honey had snapped, she drove that Volkswagen at full speed up on to the softball field where my daddy was throwing some balls around with his co-workers in the service and tried to take him out right there on the home plate. Thank God she wasn't successful in making contact, but she cleared the entire field that day! I'm certain that she felt some sense of gratification, but she was far from done with exacting her revenge. There was no reconciliation with my father and vows never meant much to Honey so as usual, she did the majority. My mother didn't need a divorce to move on, within a very short time she struck up a relationship with another guy stationed over there who she ended being with for a long while after. Honey's antics had caused such an uproar that the military contacted her and basically told her that we would have to move off base since she and my dad were not going to reconcile and the friction among the two men was a dangerous distraction. My mother tried to protest, but as a result of her shenanigans resulted in her, my brother and I had to move back to the United States to her small hometown in South Carolina. I had to start Kindergarten there, eventually the guy she started the affair with returned from active duty to his home near Dallas, Texas. He kept his promise to Honey to come and get us and set us up to start a new life there. He was actually a pretty good stepdad, but for me, he could never fill the void left by my father's absence. My dad still provided for us financially but he was an out of sight out of mind type of person. When he finally left the service he moved out to Long Beach, California. I recall there being a huge fight among my parents when he sent for me and my brother to visit. While we were out there, Sr. he had taken us to get social security cards and Honey wasn't happy at all. She swore up and down that he was up to no good, I'm not sure what his motive was, but it was undoubtedly something self-serving. He refused to answer any of her questions, that's just who Sr. is; a narcissist with a superiority complex. It wouldn't be until much later in life that I became cognizant of the blatant parallel between my relationship with my father and my marriage to Elliot Jr. Up to this day we never seemed to get back on track or had that bond that a little girl desires from her daddy. I believe that's why I was so determined to fill the gaps as a parent and in some ways, I tried to overcompensate for the fact that Suga Baby's father was killed during my pregnancy and that Sozey's daddy was a piece of shit. I met my son's father when my cousin Kitty moved to Dallas with me and Honey after graduating high school, and she and I started hanging out in the hood. For some reason, we were always drawn to street dudes. It was never serious between him and me, just a screw that turned left and I ended up with my firstborn, our son Sozey or Lil Sozey as everybody calls him. We didn't have a love connection or anything, but I was optimistic that Sozey would step up and be there for my baby. I learned early on that I was going to have to do it all on my own. Because of the way I longed for a relationship with my father, I was adamant that I would never keep my kids from their daddies intentionally. So even though Sozey never provided any financial support, whenever he did want to spend any time with Lil Sozey, I didn't have a problem with it. As a matter of fact, my son is still drawn to his father and very tight with that side of his family, especially with his grandma. She was always there for him and for me, and to this day she and I have a wonderful relationship where we talk and pray together almost every day.

Once I accepted that I couldn't rely on Big Sozey for any support, I just moved forward as if I were a single parent. I made sure Sozey was loved, educated, fresh to death. Just like I did Suga Baby when it was her time, years before when Lil Sozey turned 16 in 2010 I brought him his first car; a clean 2008 Sebring. Much like his mama, Lil Sozey has a thing for cars, he's fascinated with them, a couple of years later I also brought him a convertible Cutlass that got stolen. It's always something with that boy. I really believe that all my spoiling backfired on me and I can't tell you how many times I think of Honey and wonder if I shouldn't have followed in her footsteps as it relates to teaching Suga Baby and Sozey the value of a dollar and getting out there and getting your own.

I didn't have my own car until I was grown, and I definitely had to pay the car note, tags, and insurance. Honey wasn't trying to help me at all, her boyfriend at the time co-signed for it, but the responsibility to keep it up was on me. I was so proud, it was a brand new red 5-speed Nissan Sentra 1988, I named her "Baby", it was everything. Thank God for my mother's boyfriend, he was a doctor. He agreed to do it even though my own mother wouldn't, she knew I needed a car but wouldn't help me. I believe that her credit wasn't good enough and she just didn't want to say it.

I had gotten accustomed to her behavior by this time, yet even still to this day I am thankful for all the things that I learned from Honey, but she was a piece of work. From the time I was 14 years old, maybe even earlier than that my brother and I had to go to work with her when she would do care for in-home patients. It should come as no surprise that I made a fortune in the home health care industry because that's all I knew. Honey was a well learned, and meticulous nurse, but I was the wiz with the numbers, notes and all the admin paperwork. I typed all of my mother's notes and literally created a 200+ page policy book for our business that I wrote and typed by hand. That's how I earned my money, nothing was given to me.

My mother was a very pretty woman, and even though she was a bit overweight, she had no trouble with attracting the opposite sex. Her thing was to love em and leave em, she would joke about tapping into a man's pockets so deep that he would have to go on food stamps behind dealing with her. She did not condone laying up with a negro for free and always told me and my cousin Kitty, "You use them, don't let them use you!" As she got older, she softened her strict standards a little bit. When men weren't as affluent as she preferred, as long as they worked that was enough for her. She had to just adjust to life taking its toll on her, she had been a Rolls Royce her whole life and as she aged, Honey was more like a Mustang. Nowadays there are many things you can do to keep yourself looking young and had she been healthy enough I'm certain that she would have some form of Bariatric surgery to get her weight under control. Aside from the weight gain she always maintained her appearance, in fact on the day she passed she had been to the beauty shop. On June 23, 2007, Honey was getting ready for surgery to reduce the blockage in her aortic artery and wanted to make sure she looked her best. She was still getting around, and had even ironed my clothes that morning, we were supposed to meet at a party later. From what I understand, she was driving and pulled into a gas station, asked the manager to call 911 and said: "I'm having a heart attack." She made it back to her car and passed away at the steering wheel. That was Honey, always in the driver's seat. It's crossed my mind that I'm pretty sure had Honey still been alive I wouldn't have married Elliot Jr. She would have never accepted him as a husband for me. My mother would have shut it down and insisted that I can do so much better and she would have been right. I just thought he would have done better, he always talked about what he wanted out of life and it was so much more than where he was at the time. He was so charismatic and I had no reason to think he wasn't capable. One thing is for sure, a season of transitions was long overdue. I had to start setting boundaries for everyone in my life, not only my own children who needed to have those

-r spoons pried from their mouths but most of all for Elliot Jr. who had grown not only delusional and usurious but also malicious. I was literally sleeping with the enemy. He started taking advantage of his access to my credit and debit cards, he sold cars that I brought for him without saying anything to me about it and claimed that his jewelry had come up missing so that I could replace it. I became suspicious of his behavior and had an elaborate camera monitoring system installed throughout my home. Using an app on my phone, I could be anywhere and could see him snooping around, going through my closets, drawers and home office files. He was pathetic in every sense of the word.

As for Suga Baby and Sozey, I admit that my overzealous provisions may have stunted their self-sufficiency, but it certainly didn't handicap them. They are very talented and well mannered. They both attended top private schools and witnessed my hustle to make it happen for us. I'd hoped that would embed in them a desire to set some clear goals and get on their grind to achieve the lifestyle to which they had become accustomed, but unfortunately, instead of earning them, it drove a deep desire for having finer things in life by any means necessary. Between the allure of gaining some ridiculous street cred, Lil Sozey has always found his way back to the corners of South Dallas, slumming with the likes of his father. Thank God he's never gotten into any real trouble, but I know for a fact that he dabbles in selling marijuana and trying to be a b-boy or whatever he calls himself doing. The reality is he spends more money on smoking weed that he ever made selling it. Right now he's pursuing his interest in becoming a gangster rapper, I even sunk about $200,000 into this pipe dream until I realized that in spite of his undeniable talent, he's his own worst enemy. Now at 26 years old, he has to figure things out for himself. I can rest easy at night knowing that I gave Sozey a helluva start in life, he's armed with a whole bunch of game, a college degree and the good sense God gave him.

I had to wonder what happened to my daughter's common sense when I got the shocking news that she had gotten involved in some shit so serious that the fate of her entire future is in jeopardy and that has altered her life as we know it.

> "Sugar will sweeten anything that she touches."
>
> —Anthony T. Hincks, *American Author*

FOUR

Burnt Suga

ELLIOT JR. IS a bottom feeder, I get that, but on some level deep down inside I thought we at least had an unspoken, mutual understanding that our kids were off-limits to our fuckery. I was wrong. Of all the things he did and said to me I will never forgive or forget what he did to my Suga Baby. But let me rewind a bit and set the scene. It was the end of the Summer of 2017; I was at the office handling my business as usual when my Executive Assistant, Jozette, patched through a call. "Hello, Mrs. Jennings, this is Detective Roberts with the Dallas Police Department I need to speak to you about your daughter." At first, it didn't register that he was talking about Suga Baby; clearly, he had called my office and had stated my daughter's legal name, but I had to adjust my psyche for a moment to process that he was actually, in fact, referring to my child. He proceeded to inform me that Suga Baby was wanted in connection with a murder and robbery investigation that had recently occurred at a nearby gas station. The situation involved three African American males ages 16-17, the "alleged" assailants; and a 37-year-old Latino man, the victim. I still couldn't comprehend what in the hell that had to do with me.

Apparently, on the night of the incident, one of the older boys had entered the establishment scoping out customers and could be seen on the store's surveillance camera watching as the Latino guy paid for his stuff, then upon leaving the store, one of the boys and the other two guys approached the man to rob him. I guess things didn't go down the way they planned, if they had any plan at all, because the scene ended up bloody with an innocent young father in a body bag. I was following the detective's account very closely to gauge the connection to Suga Baby 'cause I was still clueless, but for some reason, I had a bad feeling. As he proceeded to recount the details, I was sick to my stomach and my brain was swimming around crashing against my skull. The only thing I could mutter was, "When did this take place officer?" When he said, "Friday, July 6, 2017, around 8:00 pm." I jumped out of my chair, looked at the calendar on my shelf and then again on my phone just to be sure, and blurted out "On Friday, July 6th my daughter was with me at the Big Sean concert at that time!" He asked if I could prove that, and I assured him that I most certainly could. He explained that their investigation had turned up surveillance video from multiple sources showing Suga Baby's Mustang, the piped out, impossible to miss customized car I graciously gifted to her just a year before, as the getaway car in multiple robberies and casings over the past several months. The car was registered in my name, so that's how he ended up calling me. He told me that he even had Suga Baby on camera going into the establishment to change a $20 bill into two $10 dollar bills. They believe that my daughter was scoping out the place so they could return and rob it. As far as they were concerned, she was quite possibly an integral part of this bad crew's crime spree and they wanted to speak to her immediately. I was mortified, but I agreed to meet with the detectives in person. I called but was unable to reach my Suga Baby. I knew that between concert tickets, credit card receipts and social media posts, that I could rightfully alibi her for the night of the murder, but I had no clue about the other incidents or why her car was in the middle of all of this bullshit. I reached out to her closest girlfriends but was unable to get in touch with her. In the meantime, I wanted to cooperate with the police and expedite this matter to be put to rest, so I told the detectives to meet me at my Honeycomb Hideout apartment I kept in the city for my own peace and grown folk exploits. We met up at the front door and headed to the elevator with few words exchanged. As soon as those metal doors parted, I was smacked in the face with the pungent smell of high-grade kush coming from my apartment. The aroma was so strong that we literally could have gotten a contact high just walking toward my apartment door. Between the weed and the shock of these idiots being at my apartment without my permission, I was nauseous and light-headed all at once. Trust me, there was a part of me that wanted to distract or reroute this fast-moving train wreck, but the detectives and I were only steps away from my door and although I knew that my child was on the other side, there was nothing I could do but pray.

When I opened the door, there was Suga Baby and her ride or die bestie, Lexus, and two of the knuckleheads who at this point were wanted and plastered all over the news. There was nowhere to run or hide, for any of them. For me, the worst thing was realizing that I had inadvertently brought them directly to my little girl, who had clearly grown up and gone left in a way that caught me by surprise. There were so many thoughts going through my head, I had so many questions. I asked her right then and there, "Why, Suga? You have a car, no bills, I give you money! Why would you be involved in this!?" She had the nerve to say that the money I gave her was not enough. I wanted to slap the fuck out of her and put her out of her own misery. This was my worst nightmare. I had to call her uncle, thank God Randolph II is a high-powered, well-connected attorney. But even with his far-reaching influence, Suga Baby still had to sit her little ass in jail for five long days washing out her own panties. When she was arraigned, the judge gave her three $25,000 bonds, and she wasn't working or anything so coming off that paper was all going to come down on me. My brother encouraged us to be strong and patient but assured me that he could get the amount lowered.

I must admit, Suga Baby held up pretty good for a while; she wasn't crying at first and seemed to make it through night one unscathed and in decent spirits. I think she was only able to keep it together so well because she was certain that between me and her uncle, somehow, she would be coming home the next day. I guess by the end of that long second day and she hadn't heard her name called to be released, she was starting to break down.

Come to find out, Suga started to lose it up in there when she tried calling my number and it had been changed. I had just changed my number for the 3rd time due to all of the harassing calls I was getting from Elliot Jr.'s ass and had not had a chance to give it to her, or she had not memorized it yet. Either way, the reality was starting to settle in, and Suga Baby was coming unhinged. When we finally did speak, she was crying, scared as hell and sounding so weak that I did feel for her. But more than anything I felt betrayed by her. I did everything for her, for both of my kids, I gave them a life to be envied. I did my thing as a single mother and I was grinding like a beast to keep twelve businesses afloat even in the midst of a contentious divorce. Now I had to face the fact that my baby girl was in the fight for her freedom and life as she knew it.

They let her out, but only on my brother's word and recognizance. He was very well known and respected, and his name rang bells throughout political and legal circles in the city. Her uncle had really come through for us and put his reputation on the line for her. I will forever appreciate what he did for his niece, but, boy, was I disappointed in Suga Baby. I had always trusted my daughter and now I had to face the fact that I didn't know her at all. You see, I'm not one of these delusional ass parents who think their kid's shit don't stink. I know Sozey and Suga can be a trip, and I know I spoiled them at times in my efforts to overcompensate for the fact that they didn't have a father figure in their life. Regardless of the reason, I'm not making any excuses, 'cause right is right and wrong is wrong, I'm just saying that I realize that I planted in both of my children the taste for finer things and piqued their desire to look, ride and dress a certain way, but Lord only knows I never would encourage or condone them doing some illegal shit to get it. I most definitely would never be ok with preying on hardworking folks cashing their checks or stopping to get gas. Believe you me, I was riding my daughter's ass and doing everything in my power to get to the bottom of her involvement, but I was never about to stand for anyone taking potshots at her or trying to humiliate her.

Surprise, surprise, wouldn't you know it, when Elliot Jr. heard about the situation, he slithered his ass out from under a slimy rock somewhere in the gutter and had the gall to try to do just that! I'm chilling at home on one of the few peaceful Saturday afternoons I had managed to carve out since Suga Baby's arrest when suddenly I start getting calls, texts and a bunch of annoying Facebook and Instagram notifications all at once. I noticed a call coming in from Ross, Elliot Jr.'s play nephew who was married to my girl Tangi at the time. We had all become really cool and in fact, they had named Elliot Jr. and me the godparents of their three little girls. Ross was up on Elliot's antics, but also Tangi was battling with Stage 4 cancer, so I always answered his calls. Before I could say "hey," Ross asked me if I had seen the shit on Instagram. I was clueless, not to mention Ross don't even be on social media like that, so I was still confused. He told me to brace myself and said that he thinks I needed to take a look at IG and Facebook. I quickly got off the phone with him, but before I could even pull up the app on my phone, I got a call from my ratchet ex's father, Elliot Jennings Sr., aka The Chief.

I was really tripping out at this point because I hadn't heard from Elliot Jr.'s father since before me and his low life son had entered into divorce proceedings. Although I did have some level of respect for him, and he was perhaps the most tolerable of all of Elliot Jr.'s family, we still weren't cool like that. Out of curiosity,

I answered the phone, actually distracting me from what Ross had said and all of the damn notifications that were blowing up my cell and iPad. The Chief went right for the jugular: "So, what is going with Suga Baby? I'm so disappointed in that hot tail gal! How in the hell did you let her get mixed up in all this mess?!" I was like "Excuse me? What did you…?" By this time, I was able to pull up Elliot Jr.'s Facebook page. This scumbag had not only posted my minor-aged child's mugshot but a clear photo of her car and a screenshot of the charges being filed against her. He called her a snitch and accused her of being the getaway driver in a murder, among other slanderous bullshit. I was dumbstruck at first and then overcome with rage. I proceeded to send Elliot Sr. back up under the rock he and his evil spawn belonged, hung up in his damn face and jumped into action. It's one thing to fuck with me…. but *no*body fucks with mine. You want this heat...you'd better be ready for the fire!

"Sugar should only be used to season people."

—Vera Nazarian, *The Perpetual Calendar of Inspiration*

FIVE

Eat Greedy or Choke Trying

WHEN WHEN I think of the way Elliot Jr. mishandled our marriage and all the ways he tried to play me and my children, the only punishment that feels appropriate is death. But vengeance is not mine. Lord knows if it were the retribution, I would exact on his ass would be drastic, to say the least. Was I supposed to take the high road or turn the other cheek? Hell no, he tried to take me out in more ways than one. Not only did he do everything in his power to drain my pockets and take advantage of my generosity, but he made slanderous social media posts about my daughter and threats on my life. He started a fight with Sozey that led to a physical altercation in my office, and I can't forget the way this petty mother fucker stole from me. I have his stupid ass documented on my in-home security system. Out of everything he did to me, perhaps one of the coldest is killing my dog. Yes, I said it, Elliot Jr. killed my puppy Diamond.

I had taken Suga Baby and Lil Sozey to the 2016 Olympic Games in Brazil. It was an incredible experience. I invited Elliot Jr. to go with us, but by this time he was into other things and seemed disinterested. He had only one responsibility while we were out of the country; take care of Diamond and once again he failed miserably. There was no grave marker or real explanation, he claimed she died of heat exhaustion and that he just found her dead in the kitchen near her water bowl. I'll never forget when he told me the news I was in the airport in Rio and had just told him what time to pick us up and he just blurted it out. "Uh, uh, Diamond died". It was like I was suspended in motion. I could see all the travelers moving past us and watched as Sozey and Suga Baby bickered over some Beats headphones, but I couldn't move or make out any noises. The sound of his disgusting deep voice snapped me out of my haze, "Keilanii! Keilanii! Do you hear me? I said I was sorry about your damn dog, but if you just gone give a nigga the silent treatment then it ain't shit I can do." I just hung up the phone and pulled myself together so my kids and I could get through this 13-hour flight back to Dallas. I couldn't bear telling them what had happened to Diamond or let that fuck with them on the plane ride the way I knew it was hurting me.

We loved that dog, losing Diamond was like losing a beloved member of the family. I figured it would be easier to break the news when they landed. The crazy thing is when we arrived in the US and went through customs, Sozey was detained and arrested. I was mortified; apparently, he had a warrant for an old probation violation that I knew nothing about. I was outdone, Suga Baby and I went home, and Elliot Jr. went back to pick up Sozey from the airport jail once he was processed. At that point, the drama of Sozey's untimely arrest overshadowed the trauma of Diamond's untimely demise. I let Elliot break the news about the dog to them, and I took a valium and crawled in my oversized king bed.

Whenever I would think that that the drama had died down, or that Elliot Jr. couldn't get any worse, he always managed to stoop even lower than even I believed he was capable of. I started hearing from Ross and a number of other sources that my ex was defaming my mother's character and memory. By this point, I had grown accustomed to hearing from people torrid allegations of him sleeping with members of my staff, close friends, sisters, and cousins. To this very day, I believe many of the rumors, but for this low life to actually go around boasting that he had screwed Honey was low even for him. I was seething when I found out from Suga Baby that he had hinted at this to her. I guess he called himself tearing us down when he said to her directly, "You better watch yourself, lil girl, you don't want to turn out like your mama. She or your grandma ain't all they portray themselves to be. Shit, you know me, and Honey got really close back in the day, that was my baby too!" Suga Baby was thoroughly disgusted and perplexed, my poor child held onto his toxic words for days until I finally got her to open up to me. She called herself protecting my feelings and had suppressed the awful things he said about us. What kind of asshole stoops to such depths? I honestly think he believes that stories of these kinds of exploits make him look good. He's walking around poking out his chest like he's the man because he claims to have screwed me over and screwed all the women that mean something to me. All I can say is even this evil nigger must have an angel on his shoulder because he's long overdue for Karma to kick his sorry black ass, in the worst way. My wet dream of him being six feet under has not quite come to pass, so I take some pleasure in the fact that he is sick to his stomach knowing that I gave his nephew Ross, who we call Baby Boy, an all-access pass to Sugarland.

Elliot Jr. and Baby Boy aren't actually related, but they grew up around one another and were extremely close. Ross, several years younger, looked up to Elliot Jr. and referred to him as his uncle. Over the years they remained tight and hung out together watching sports and probably asses at the bars around town. I met Ross and his wife, Tangi, through Elliot Jr., and we all grew pretty cool over the years. Tangi and Ross each had a daughter prior to hooking up, and together had two girls. When their oldest, China Doll, was born in 2011, they asked Elliot Jr. and me to be the godparents. A few years later they had Boogie, and we fell in love with her and right in place playing a loving role in their lives.

Even when shit started going downhill for Elliot Jr. and me, I still was active in Ross and Tangi's children's' lives. Not to mention Suga Baby had grown extremely close to them and they looked up to her as a big god-sister and stayed latched on to her hip. Tangi was a good mother and a good wife, I respected the fact that she was always trying to make a better life for her family. I love to see people making an effort to do something positive. Tangi wasn't afraid of hard work, she was a medical assistant and was very dedicated to advancing even throughout her illness. She had been sick for a couple of years; discovering that she had breast cancer. Tangi was a fighter and made the decision to have a mastectomy and go through chemo and radiation. She was in remission for a while and was still pushing forward and being the best mom she could be, but when cancer came back, it came back viciously. The disease had metastasized all over her brain, lungs, and legs, all over really, it had gotten worse. I didn't realize just how poorly her health had deteriorated until I brought her out to Las Vegas with me in 2017 when I flew out all my girls to celebrate my birthday; Sugar Mama style. Although Tangi put up a brave face, it was clear throughout the trip that she was very weak and had to be in a wheelchair the entire time. After a while, she couldn't stand at all. I knew then that I had to do more as a friend. I had pulled back from coming around because of Elliot Jr. At the time he and I were in the throes of our divorce battles and I just didn't want to run into him over there. Plus, my ex was not one of Tangi's favorite people; she couldn't stand him at times. She knew how he tried to get over on me; as far as she was concerned, he was a low life and always getting Ross caught up in some bullshit. Still, I felt bad for not helping out more like picking up the girls, and I'm sure I could have communicated better, but again I called myself trying to spare Tangi and Ross the antics of Elliot Jr. and at any moment he might just stop by their place. He wasn't the "call before you come" type, so I stayed away to avoid bringing any negativity or bad vibes their way. However, once I understood the dire state of Tangi's health, I made it up in my mind that I would do anything I could to help them out no matter what, so if that meant bumping into Satan himself, then oh well, so be it.

I checked in on China Doll, Boogie and the older girls more often, I visited Tangi as much as possible, as she was in the hospital at this point. I took food over to the house and was as resourceful as possible for all of them during this tough time. As hard as it was for me to accept, I could tell that she was transitioning. I'd worked in-home health care and hospice for most of my life and I knew the inevitable was near. Tangi passed away right before our divorce was finalized, the day before Suga Baby and I were leaving for our European vacation. So, when Ross called, I sprung into action making arrangements and doing all that I could to get the ball rolling for her homegoing services. The actual funeral was about a week later, Suga Baby and I were in Italy at the time, but our thoughts, love, and prayers were with them and I knew the real work would begin when the services were over. I resolved that I would best honor Tangi's legacy by loving her kids. I was and will forever be the godmother to those girls and just like I did it by myself with Suga and Sozey, I was perfectly prepared to serve as the sole Godparent with or without Elliot Jr. During this time, he was rate because he was starting to realize that things weren't going to go the way he wanted in the dissolution of our sham of a marriage. He was starting to come apart at the seams because I had secretly cut him off, trying to put pressure to get him back in court to combat his ridiculous stall tactics. Being on a 5-star vacation in Europe served its purpose to help me avoid Elliot Jr. because I knew he would have his ass at that funeral. Certainly, if we were in the States, we would not have missed it.

As the weeks and months progressed following Tangi's passing, more than ever I was committed to moving on and living my best possible existence. I was helping Sozey pursue his rap artist aspirations, supporting Suga Baby with her championship cheer team and making certain that she got out of high school and into somebody's college the same as her big brother had. Me and Baby Boy's relationship started to strengthen organically. Not only had he come to rely on me heavily to help out with the girls, but he brought him and the girls a comfortable little home much closer to me, making it more convenient for them to spend time and do things with Suga Baby and me.

One day Elliot Jr. stopped by Ross' to drop off some drapes for the living room that he had hemmed at his upholstery shop. It had been a minute since he had come by; in fact, months had passed since Tangi's funeral and ain't no telling what he had heard through the grapevine. From what I understand, he started to pick and prod Baby Boy a little, trying to get a gauge on me and his nephew's dynamic. He knew that we were cool, but he didn't know the extent of the friendship. Soon enough he found out that Baby Boy and I were dating; he was heated and green with envy. At first, he tried to act like it didn't faze him but more and more his fury started to show. He ran his mouth like a little bitch and even went on another social media tirade making comments under a photo of Baby Boy, Suga Baby and me hanging out with the girls. The post read "Awww such a lovely family, that's what I'm talking about. Eat greedy, Nephew!" Clearly, he was encouraging Baby Boy to use me the way he had. Ross found it amusing and wanted to just blow it off. I saw no humor in it and I found it very humiliating and disrespectful. I was infuriated and I wanted Baby Boy to check his ass in a real way. If he wasn't going to deal with him, I was going to take it to the streets. Baby Boy calmed me down and reasoned with me to accept that Elliot's comments or opinions have no bearing on our relationship. He pointed out that I had too much at stake and too much to lose. He reminded me of where he's from, and how he's cut. If he were to step to his uncle, there would be serious consequences and repercussions for Elliot Jr. and that it would get ugly. He recommended that we just allow him to wallow in his own self-pity. Baby Boy knows him best and understood how to get at him, so in this circumstance, I deferred to his approach, but for me, his "eat greedy" comment was proof that he had set out to use me and yet another documented infraction that Elliot Jr. would one day be held accountable for. If it was the last thing I ever did, I would see him pay. I would show that nigger how to eat greedy alright, I would take a bite out of his ass that I would live to savor for decades to come. After that incident, Ross pretty much cut off all ties to Elliot Jr. He, I and my Goddaughters kept it moving. I admit that I had many reservations, guilt and felt bad at first for engaging intimately with Ross. Tangi and I were close, I loved her, and I love her girls. Dating her husband was never my intention, but I have come to terms with it. To be honest, I fucks with Ross, but it only goes so far. I don't put nothing past him or any nigga. Little do he know, I'm got a hold to his Apple watch on a fluke and came across some shady dialogue between him and some hood rat bitch. At this point, it takes a lot more to ruffle my feathers. I stay on guard but ain't nothing like being aware of what I am dealing with. We still kick it and have a good time, and I will always have those girls' backs, on the strength of Tangi alone, but make no mistake about it. Sugar has her eye on the prize and her sights set for something and someone so much bigger and better than Elliot Jr. and Baby Boy combined. Please believe, if Sugar ever let her guard down again, it would be for a boss, a bona fide Sugar Daddy who could not only pay his way but exceed my contributions. But let's face it, I have it going on, so I already know that's not going to be easy. One thing's for certain and two things for sure, the last thing I would ever let happen again is to fall for a needy negro looking to eat greedy off of me. I WOULDN'T EVEN GIVE HIM THE CHANCE TO CHOKE WHILE TRYING!

"Don't cry, Treasure. You'll get me all wet and then I'll melt. I'm made of sugar, don't you know."

—Kady Cross, *The Girl in the Steel Corset*

SIX

I Love the KKK

KITTY ARRIVED IN Dallas, Texas, with nothing but a passed down baby blue pleather suitcase and $18 to her name. She had just graduated from her Charleston South Carolina high school, class of 1988, and had no intention of ever going back. Honey took her in with no hesitation; my mother always treated her nieces and nephews as her own kids. Prior to Kitty coming to live with us at the time, she would stay with us every summer, so we were very close. Kitty is my mother's brother's second daughter. She was 18 at the time, I'm older than her by only one year. Her mom and Honey were pregnant together two years in a row. So, although she is my first cousin, she's more like a sister to me.

At the time Kitty arrived that fall, I had gone back

up to school, so she slept in my room. When I was home, she either slept with me or my mother, but it was all good because we made it work. Whenever I did get away from campus, we picked up like we never left off and did a lot of partying. Kitty was a very pretty redbone, skinny with long silky hair and, boy, did she love to flaunt her looks. Don't get me wrong, I had my fun and I liked to fool around here and there but Kitty was hot in the pants. My cousin loved sex and the men loved her. To her, it was all fun and games as long as the drinks, food and lavish lifestyle kept coming. Kitty didn't give a damn if a nigga was a dope boy, a credit card scammer or a married old man with five kids, all she cared about was getting fucked, and whenever possible, getting paid. The problems came into play when these cheating dudes' wives came looking for her ass. Come to find out that's what sparked her unannounced arrival on our doorstep that summer. Women started coming to her momma's house with their snotty-nosed babies in tow looking for Kitty's blood and that wasn't going over too well with her folks, so she had to get out of Dodge. I never judged my cousin, we just hung out and did our thing. That was her lifestyle, she liked street cats and hustle boys with paper and was pretty enough to attract them and get what she wanted from them so I could never be mad about that. I always held my own too, so we were a force to be reckoned with. Kitty was, as they say, young, dumb and full of cum in search of a fun time and a better life and I was along for the ride; as they say, "I was with the shits!"

We kicked it every night, sometimes I would go to work if not at both jobs, at least one then we would party until daybreak, I'd rush in to take a shower and go right back to work. I'd get off, get dressed, go drinking in the club and out to eat afterward. Still to this day, I don't know how I survived that crazy routine. Kitty was going with this big-time drug dealer named Red; he was one of the first and few to have a cell phone, we would be all on it calling people like we were the shit. Well, technically we were the shit and you couldn't tell us any differently. Red would give Kitty money to shop, and his friends would call themselves liking me or whatever and would give me money to cop clothes, bags, shoes, and stuff so we did in high fashion. Me and Kitty was kicking it so hard that it became a real problem. I couldn't keep up with my course work at Richland Junior College, I kept missing classes and pretty much just quit. Yeah yeah, I know, my smart ass flunked out of community college. But please believe Sugar eventually got herself all the way together and registered at Southern Methodist University, but I had to cut a lot of that hanging and shit out. I always knew my end game and that to achieve many of my goals I had to be well educated and credentialed. I loved for guys to give me money, but I was more excited about being the Head Bitch In Charge and calling the shots. It cost to be the boss and I was willing to pay, so I had to get a couple of degrees under my Versace belt!

As for Kitty, school was never her thing. She tried for a brief stint at junior college and other trade schools but that wasn't for her. She was more of a worker bee; she could do a job, but she wasn't the student type. I think on some level she truly believed that she could get by on her looks. She typically had several men at a time, and as I pointed out, she ain't never had no qualms about having multiple partners or sleeping with someone's husband. None of that was out of her comfort zone. It worked for her for a while until she met Bobby.

My cousin just knew she had hit the jackpot when she started fooling around with this slick-talking negro. Bobby was the purse man and she thought he had a little something, so she messed around and had a baby by him. That move totally backfired in her face; he went from giving her purses to her having to pay for them. His good for nothing ass got her. He seemed to be a pretty decent father but as Kitty's man, he wasn't shit. Not only would he stick his dick in any bitch that bought one of his designer knockoffs, but he had the nerve to be an abusive hypocrite. I remember one summer Bobby had heard that Kitty was fucking around with this old guy in the neighborhood. She got dressed up all sexy, he picked her up, took her down to the lake and beat her ass. Truth be told, she was cheating with that man, but he didn't have to do her like that. She had a black eye on the left and busted vessel in her right eye. I don't know how she talked herself out of that situation, but somehow, she made it out alive. They only stayed together for a couple more years. Other than being mean to my cousin at times, I really didn't have any problems with Bobby; in fact, it was him that told me that Elliot Jr. was going around bragging how he had slept with Kitty and how she was smiling all up in my face while stabbing me in my back. I'm not going to lie, that was a tough pill to swallow because in spite of her slutty ways, I love her, and I would ride for her till the wheels came off. I've always been down for Kitty; I was in the delivery room when she had both of her sons. As I said, she was more like a sister, and my mother loved her to death. I think Honey felt like she needed to take her under her wings maybe because she saw areas where her parents were lacking. Her father paid child support and was somewhat present in her life, but he wasn't like an active hands-on dad offering support and validation, so maybe that's what she was seeking in all those men. Whether she has ever been diagnosed or not, Kitty is a sex addict. I used to try to talk to her about it or try to tell her that she deserved better, but she would dismiss my concerns and explain "I just like sex". I think she believes her sexual behavior is normal, but her promiscuity is anything but normal. She's had a lot of wear and tear on her body, which resulted in certain permanent ailments. I'll just leave it at that for now. All I know is the things you do coming up have a way of catching up with you and Lord only knows that you won't be able to bend over and drop it like it's hot all of your life and not expect to catch on fire.

When Kitty turned 24, I guess she called herself settling down and finding some level of stability. She reconnected with a blue-collar type of guy she knew from her hometown named Mickey. He was a few years older than Kitty and worked for his uncle at his auto parts store in Tallahassee, Florida. He seemed like a decent man with good intentions and aspirations in spite of the fucked-up cards he was dealt early on in life. From what I heard, his mother had shot his daddy and then killed herself while he and his little sister were in the car. He had come to Dallas to visit his Aunt Nadine who was here, and that's how he and Kitty had linked up after so many years. So, in '95 or '96, Mickey and Kitty got engaged. She had always dreamed of a big, fancy wedding but didn't have money like that and her parents certainly weren't in the position to help her with anything or contribute financially whatsoever. Even though her parents have five kids between them, her mother kept her plate full of even more children. She was a serial foster parent who wasn't especially compassionate but used that as her reason to not work. She was barely surviving on checks from the state, so she had nothing to contribute to Kitty and Mickey's nuptials. Her father had a job, but he was a womanizer who wasn't really all that invested in Kitty. His saving grace was his big sister Honey, who not only stepped up to come to her favorite niece's rescue but reveled in the chance to show off. That was my mother, she would help you, but rest assured everyone else is going to know about it. I'm sure that every distant cousin from the dirty south to the shores of the East Coast knew that we had paid for Kitty's elaborate wedding. It was a picture-perfect affair at the Regency Grand in downtown Dallas. Unfortunately, the family gossip and credit card bills endured longer than Kitty and Mickey's marriage. As the saying goes, "You can't turn a hoe into a housewife," poor Mickey learned that the hard way. I knew my cousin couldn't help herself when it came to her craving for sex and fucking different men, but I had hoped that when they moved down to Florida to start their life together, she would clean up her act when she became a wife. From what I heard, her compulsion to feed her carnal desires had gotten so extreme that one day when Mickey popped up to the house to surprise his wife with some flowers, he got the surprise of his life. He drove up and noticed a UPS truck in his driveway. Annoyed that he couldn't pull in, he walked up to the driver's side and lo and behold he was the one who got the surprise! Mickey's little homemaker was signing for the UPS driver's package with her mouth. Needless to say, Kitty's hot ass ended up back in Dallas and on my couch. I never judged my cousin, but I hoped that she would slow down and get her act together.

We remained close and she helped me out with my son. In fact, Sozey and her son Darren were close in age and always hung together. I love my baby cousin, who is more like a nephew to me, but he was always in and out of trouble with the law. Years later when Kitty had hooked up with this dude from North Dallas for a stint and had just moved in with him, Darren actually had a police standoff at her house. His crazy-ass tried to rob a Cricket Wireless store in Mesquite, Texas. There were cameras and everything; he tried to get them to open the register, but the cashier tripped the alarm. By the time he made it out of the parking lot, the Mesquite Police and Texas Highway Patrol were on his ass. He wasn't too far from the house his momma was staying at with her new man, so he drove over there, ran inside the house and barricaded himself. We are a close-knit family and when he called me in the midst of the chase, I kept a cool head because my only mission was to keep my nephew alive. The cops had tracked him down to the house and were treating it as a high-risk standoff situation. Darren was super hyper, pacing the floor and describing the scene to me. He would move the blinds to the side and go on about how many police cars were pulling up. When he told me that the Dallas SWAT team had pulled up on the lawn, I instantly felt sick to my stomach. I stayed on the phone with him and very calmly explained to him why it wasn't worth risking his life and that situations like this don't turn out well. I reminded him that he has his entire life ahead of him and that his family is going to always love and be there for him. Once I got his attention, I encouraged him to get something to eat and to make sure he had on a sweatshirt and to lay flat on the floor when the police came up the stairs. I told him that I loved him, that he was better than this, and that we are going to deal with this as a family. Darren had previously been charged with Aggravated Robbery and Burglary of a Habitat in 2009, Aggravated Assault with a Deadly Weapon in 2014 and with this final straw he racked up another Aggravated Robbery charge. They considered Kitty's son as a menace to society and gave him 10 years in a federal penitentiary.

Kitty was really messed up behind Darren's ordeal with the law, but she never talked about it much. She stayed with ole boy for a while, but eventually, that came to an end. Over the years she was off and on with several guys but nothing too serious. She was still sleeping around with every Tom, Dick, and Harry, but truly I never thought for a second that she would ever cross the line with my man. I'll never forget the day she called me to give me a heads up that Bobby was going to be calling to tell me about a rumor that she and Elliot Jr. were messing around. She prefaced it by saying that I know that my older sis Kairo is always keeping up some shit and that these allegations were sparked up by her. Sure enough, Bobby hit my line and told me all about what Kairo had told him in so-called confidence. He said that Kairo sounded distraught and that she couldn't keep it to herself any longer. Everybody knows that my sister is a bit of an emotional mess, and to say that she is overly dramatic would be an understatement. According to Bobby,

Kairo said she knew firsthand that Kitty and Elliot had been fooling with one another and that she knew that Kitty was not to be trusted. At the time me and Kairo were somewhat on the outs, so I guess that's why she didn't call me herself. On the other hand, I know my sister felt some kind of way about how close Kitty and I had gotten over the years. So, when I ran into Kitty and asked her about what Bobby said about her fucking my husband, she was appalled and said that she would confront Elliot Jr. directly and that she wanted to kick Bobby's ass for spreading these vicious lies. I knew Kitty had easily slept with 150 to 200 men, but I didn't want to believe that even within her sex addiction that she would stoop to sleeping with my husband.

For now, our relationship is fine, we remain cordial and I still only want the best for her. She's snagged another sucker to put a ring on it and they attended my "Fabulous 50th" destination birthday extravaganza in New Orleans. As far as I know, they are happy and as always, I wish the best for her. I just put the allegations that Elliot Jr. made in the back of my mind because I don't have any proof so I'm not going to kill a relationship over an unsubstantiated rumor. Not to mention, Sugar's life is so sweet, and I don't have time to worry myself over it, I'll just let Karma deal with her. If Kitty did add my husband as a notch on her oversized belt, then she has to live with her own guilt. When I think about Elliot Jr., not only is he capable of cheating, stealing and tarnishing my daughter's reputation, but I have no doubt that he could sleep with a friend or family member. Little did I know just how low he would go in his efforts to try to hurt me. Not only did he brag about sleeping with Kitty, but he ended up doing so under oath, in front of a jury of his peers and for the whole world to hear. The killer part is that he also threw my sister Kairo and my best friend Keisha under the bus right along with her ass!

KEISHA

Much like Kitty, my best friend Keisha also had a strong affinity for screwing around. Unlike Kitty, she was formally diagnosed as a sex addict. Another difference between Keisha and Kitty is that Keisha tends to fall hard and get married to one of her lovers and shuts down shop for a while. When I really stop and think about it, Keisha's always been in search of some kind of validation from a man. Her father was present for most of her life, but he was more focused on his other family that consisted of his wife and little girl. Keisha's mother was a piece of work. The crazy thing is that she is literally a math and science genius who had been on and off again on drugs for most of Keisha's life. I was also very fond of her mother and considered her an auntie. She was brilliant and traveled all over the world with good-paying jobs, ut she couldn't get that monkey off of her back. To this day she's still one of the smartest people you'd ever meet, but now she makes Fire Sticks with all the classic and latest movies. For $99 she will hook you up.

I always felt for Keisha and her situation with her parents, so we bonded from the time we met in the 8th grade, in Dallas. For the most part, our friendship has stood the test of time. We used to talk like every day, but she's been married five or six times and during those relationships, for some reason, we lose touch. I get it, in her mind she needed to shut me out of her life to focus on the life she was trying to manufacture. I was cool with that and I wanted her to be happy and to attain the life and the love that she was so desperate for. She was notorious for sleeping with negros that she thought she could make love her but other than an occasional lay, she never heard from most of them again. See I never judged her or cared even, and I would never allow anyone to openly pass judgment on my bestie. Honey used to say, "He who brings a bone, carries a bone." So basically, when folks were coming at me with dirt about Keisha, I would just shut them down. It would irritate me that she doesn't do the same when it comes to me. Over the years I know for a fact that she would allow other people to say things about me, 'cause a lot of times she would be the one to tell me what was said. When I would check her about the conversation, she would say that she defended me or iced them out, but I don't feel like she did enough, and I could never shake the feeling that she was as much a party to the gossip as the other haters. Still, we are close, our youngest children are around the same age. We understood each other a lot, especially when we were younger. We shared similar aspirations and careers, so we were on the same path and she was very close to my family and was treated as a sister and we certainly share secrets as sisters do.

As we got older, Keisha hung out with a more collegiate crowd, especially when Kitty came to live with us. Me and Kitty gravitated more to street dudes and partying, while Keisha was into more blue-collar or strait-laced guys. She did well in her studies and graduated from the U of T with bachelor's and master's degrees. Like her mom, Keisha has always been bright, but with that came this air about her that she was smarter than everyone else. She's an independent CPA, and would always keep a job, but with her, it was always something. She never seemed to fit into Corporate America" nor did she want to for that matter. But she often complained about not fitting into the white-washed culture as a strong black woman and she would rant about working vs conforming. She wanted to be Afrocentric in a white man's world, but her specialty is tax accounting. Her black ass ended up working at the IRS of all places. It was a great paying position, but she much preferred working independently than in a strict, 9 to 5 environment. I've always admired her accounting knowledge and passion for her craft and over the years I've relied on her services. Keisha worked with me for several of my businesses. When my first home health care business dissolved, she helped me through it with her expertise. We took a break in working together back in 2006 while I was growing my business and we maintained a relatively tight relationship.

Although we talked pretty regularly and spent some of the holidays together, we didn't really hang out in the traditional sense since high school. Over the years she was going through so many men I didn't get to meet them all. When she would come to my parties, she would maybe meet a guy I was dealing with. So, I was in no rush to introduce her to Elliot Jr. Even still, when they finally did meet, I don't think she thought much of him. She was married at the time and dealing with a lot, but when she got divorced again, she would come around more and got to see a different, more charming side of him. They developed somewhat of a cool friendship and eventually, she even started to prepare his tax returns. When she married her last husband, though, for some reason he couldn't stand Elliot Jr. It was serious. I could never put my finger on it, but it was almost like he knew something, or just had a bad vibe. One thing's for sure, he did not fool with Elliot Jr. and Keisha let me know that.

Lord only knows I had so much on my plate most of the time that I had zero energy to invest in trying to figure that out. Moreover, Keisha was going through a lot at the time; she had some issues, to say the least, but considering her background, to me it was understandable. To her credit, I must say that she did make efforts to improve herself and get some grounding in her life. She was always enrolling herself in self-improvement groups, classes, counseling and seminars on everything from overeating to sex addiction. She had trouble with short term memory, so she even went through a brain training series. It must have been frustrating to be on this constant quest for personal growth, but never fully achieve it. As much as she tried, it was as if she could never find a balance or a sense of normalcy. She was involved in her son's football career, in between husbands, and then it was the time that she started fooling with this married barber. She even confided in me that one day he pulled up outside her office with his wife in the car, telling her that he had to run in to get some paperwork from his accountant. They had sex while his wife waited in the car—when it came to sex, Keisha was emotionally void. Keisha demonstrated her propensity to just screw a man with no meaning time and time again. During my 40th birthday, my girls took me out, booked a suite and hired this fine ass Puerto Rican male exotic dancer. We were having a good time, lots of laughs and drinks, but for me and the rest of the women, that's where it ended—a fun night to celebrate me! But not for Keisha and Kitty, they turned fucking that stripper into a conquest.

Early the next morning when she made the walk of shame to my suite for coffee she said: "Shiiitt...ain't no shame in my game, I had to beat Kitty to that piece!" I just laughed, shook my head and sipped on some hot tea, literally. Kitty, on the other hand, was fuming!

For the longest while, she spent a lot of her spare time running through this motorcycle club in South Dallas dating or screwing whomever. I don't know if it was a self-esteem issue or what, but she wasn't a bad looking woman. She had cocoa brown skin, was super thick, wore designer glasses and a weave. Most of all I can say that she has a beautiful soul. She is no Sugar, but she can hold her own. I never got the impression that she saw me as competition, I think she knew that I was way out of her league both personally and professionally.

Aside from her work as a CPA, she wrote a self-help book. It was an Amazon bestseller, which was a huge milestone for her, I guess. I never saw any promotions or marketing so I can't imagine it being very successful. There was no tour unless you count her Dallas book signing, I went to it along with Kitty, Kairo, and about ten other people. Keisha likes to think of herself as a teacher, educator, and author, so she gives a seminar on maintaining a budget or something in the self-help space, I don't know. Hell, if you remember I do. I didn't always get it, but I supported her. I attended one and I co-sponsored another one, still, she only had like three to four attendees. I just shook my head, some people see themselves on some grandiose platform or put this idea in their brain that they are already there, but take it from me, you truly have to crawl before you walk. I'm not so sure that Keisha ever wanted to put in the work, so I couldn't understand how she expected to take it to the next level, which made no sense to me. I'm the type of person and friend who so much as tells you so. I'm known for being brutally honest, and I feel like deep down that's why Keisha resented me, and perhaps why she became subject to Elliot Jr.'s treachery.

So, one Friday a couple of years back, I am at my desk starting to pack up stuff, at the time Keisha was working for me, and we had just got back from a late lunch at PF Chang's at Northpark Mall. I had to go out that way to pick up a limited-edition Versace bag that I had ordered and my favorite Guerlain perfume from Saks. As I'm getting things together, I couldn't shake this nagging feeling that Keisha's energy had been a bit off earlier that afternoon. So, just as I'm about to log out of my desktop, I started getting all of these notifications and pings on both my computer and my phone. I was like WTF? I clicked on one of the notifications and it took me to a post that Elliot Jr. had made. By this time, we were totally on the outs and in the throes of our contentious divorce, but clearly, he had decided to go below the belt. All the activity and buzz were actually people tagging me and making comments about his cryptic post. He basically said that he had "love for the KKK" and that he had slept with every one of them. His post read something like, "Folks wanna call me the enemy...little do they know I'm sleeping with the enemy that they so quick to call friends and family, ha ha sucker!" This ignorant nigga was such a liar and narcissist that I really didn't take it beyond face value. As far as I was concerned this was another of his feeble attempts to hurt, humiliate and throw me off my square. He knew that this would get back to me and that I was well aware that he referred to my closest friend, Keisha, my cousin Kitty and my sister Kario as the "KKK". He was just making himself look like a fool and a delusional, vicious liar. It wasn't until a few days later that I actually started to consider that there may be some actual truth to his statements.

So that Sunday, Baby Boy and I had met up for me to drop off my goddaughters to him; I had taken them out to celebrate the youngest girl's birthday. We were just chopping it up a bit while they were putting away all the new toys, bags of clothes and other stuff that their god mommy had showered them with. By now I knew he had seen the post, everybody in our circle had, so I was like "What is wrong with your people, why is he out here slandering and lying on folks like that?" Baby Boy hunched up his shoulders and gave me this eyebrow-raised look and proceeded to tell me that Elliot Jr. had confided in him a while back that he actually had messed with Kitty once, and that he had been fucking around with Keisha off and on for years. Baby Boy stood there with his head lowered and confessed that he even heard her on the phone himself at one point and that Elliot Jr. showed him a burner phone that she got him apparently so that she could keep in touch with him. I can't lie, that shit kinda stung a bit. I always defended those bitches to him, and I had their backs through thick and thin. Elliot used to say that people didn't really like me like that, and he would try to use that to tear me down. He said over and over again that Keisha was never really my friend.

One time me Sozey and Suga Baby had gone out to California to visit my Sr. for Father's Day. Out of nowhere, Elliot Jr. sent me this long text saying: "When people get mad at you they call me and tell me the shit that you say about me, you bout as stupid as the bitches you call your friend and talk shit about me too." I'm baffled thinking, I'm out having a good time with your daddy and he hit me with this shit? I just blew it off, but in hindsight, I recall that about a week before Keisha and I had words behind her expecting me to cover all of her costs for a New York trip we were planning. As my accountant working so closely with my finances and knowing all the leisure spending I did, Keisha automatically assumed that I should come out of my pockets for her to live lavishly. Shoot, I had already covered the plane tickets and the hotel, but she was expecting me to buy her tickets to the shows and other excursions we had planned.

Anyway, when I got home, I had sent a carefully constructed message to the KKK. I knew exactly what I was doing, it read, "I can't believe this shit! I'd expect this from a dog ass nigga, he gone try to shoot his shot, but messing with my friends? My family? Who is really that desperate for dick and low down enough to sleep with my husband? I bet you thought he wasn't gone ever tell me about your nasty ass...smh that goes to show that just when you think you know somebody they will smile in your face and stab a knife right in your back!" Like clockwork Keisha and my sister, Kairo responded immediately. My sister was on the way over anyway, so she ended up pulling into my driveway a few seconds later in a tizzy. I was unpacking my suitcases from California when Kairo came in all flustered and sweating, trying to assure me that Elliot Jr. had got the wrong K if he called himself talking about her. She was in tears trying to convince me that she would never do anything so dirty. After watching her squirm and her eyes pop of her head for damn near 30 mins, I had to put her out of her misery. I said, "Oh girl, I must have sent that to the wrong K, that wasn't directed at you". I continued to put my things away and acted like I was so unfazed, but I knew the seed was planted and that her propensity for gossip and drama would bloom wildly and that she alone would have the others "K's" shaking in their boots. Keisha had texted me like five times before she couldn't take my silence anymore and took to calling me. When I finally answered her call, she went on and on about how she can't stand Elliot Jr. and how she refused to even dignify his accusations with a response. I must admit she held it together, but I know her, and I could see that on the inside she was coming apart at the seams. Her mother was on one of her stressful relapses and she needed her job and didn't want anything to come between her and her paycheck. The only person who I didn't speak with directly was Kitty; when she feels some form of guilt, she tends to shut down, I've seen her do it before. The next day or so she sent a text that read "I don't know what's wrong with Elliot Jr. Cuz, he's crazy, I love you." Just as I told Keisha and Kario, I simply responded by saying "Oh girl, my bad I didn't even mean to send that to you, I guess I have too many K's in my phone. Time to purge."

Me, Kitty and Kario kept it pushing, for the most part, I just keep my eyes peeled and decided that without actual proof I wasn't going to let him take my piece of mind or those relationships from me the way he had tried to take so much else. But for some odd reason, me and Keisha never seemed to get back on the same page. Our business relationship suffered too after a while, so we are on a pause due to different things, mainly business. When I really stop and think about it, she probably did get down with Elliot Jr. I get it that's what sex addicts do. But what kills me is how she now calls herself a life coach and relationship expert but can't keep her shit together. She not only flops from job to job and husband to husband but she struggles with her health and weight. It was always something with her, she even had lap band surgery to help battle her obesity but found a way to trick it and would still eat like a pig. In spite of all of her degrees, certifications, and distinctions, it still didn't add up to happiness or true fulfillment, I guess life just has a way of balancing the books on people, especially CPAs.

KAIRO

I can't talk about the KKK without elaborating on my older sister Kairo. She's quite a special case. We have the same mother, but Honey let her go live with her father in Abbeville, South Carolina, where she was raised until she was 19. For the most part, she had a normal childhood until being sexually abused by a cousin from the age of 9 until she was 13. I believe that violation of her innocence and peace of mind really affected her in a deep, psychological way. By the time she came to live with me and my Honey at the age of 19, she was an emotional basket case who cried and acted out at the drop of a dime. Her inability to heal or push past it and the overall juvenile behavior have to some degree rendered her ineffective in functioning as an adult. She's lived her adult life co-dependent on the system, welfare, food stamps, and public housing to survive. She was never much of a looker, so it's not like she could rely on her feminine wiles to land a man to take care of her. Don't get me wrong, she's not repulsive or anything; she has light skin, overly large breasts, with very pretty hair, but she's always battled with obesity, suffered from severe insecurity, low self-esteem, and anxiety. Whenever there's ever any contention, she behaves like a child and demonstrates how emotionally unstable she really is. Did I mention that she cries at the drop of a dime? OMG, I love my sister, but she can be such a basket case. One thing Kairo is good at is saving money. I swear she will hoard a coin and can turn $1 into $10. She lived with me for three years and never paid a cent, so when I finally asked her to leave, I couldn't understand why she got so upset 'cause I knew she must have as several bands tucked in that worn mattress of hers. Not to mention when she so much as took my baby to get some chicken nuggets, she didn't hesitate to let me know about it and took being reimbursed her $4.56 very seriously. I appreciate the times she's looked out for my kids, but I had to pay her. I know she loves Suga Baby and Sozey, but being their aunt most definitely benefited her financially. Living with us was helpful at times but it helped her more 'cause she didn't have any expenses.

I know she didn't like it when Elliot Jr. came to live with us, but what could she really say? Overall, I believe she thought he was okay, but she and no one else expected me to marry him. At one point, he and I were scheduled to have a big, grand wedding, so our random Vegas wedding took everyone by storm, especially Kario, I believe she was more concerned about how our marriage was going to impact her living situation. On the other hand, I know she secretly thought that I could do better, but she never has been in the position to say anything. For a long time, us all living in the house together didn't really cause any friction, our house was big enough. But after a while, it seemed like the walls were closing in.

It got to the point where she couldn't stand Elliot Jr., not only was he an asshole to me and my son at different times but as his true colors started to show; he would be in my office snooping around, looking through my files and bank statements trying to figure out how much money I was making. He was always so greedy and ungrateful and by Kairo living with us, she witnessed the BS and that left a bad taste in her mouth. I knew the disdain that Kairo had developed for Elliot Jr, that's why when all the allegations about him sleeping with the "KKK" hit the net, I found it really hard to believe that she could ever sleep with him. But you never know; her way of thinking never quite made sense to me anyway, so on some level, it could have been her way of trying to end the relationship by proving to me what a dog he is. The crazy thing is, knowing how her brain works, this wouldn't be so farfetched.

More than my lack of tolerance for my sister's antics and childish behavior is for her lack of loyalty. Time and time again, she's continued to deal with and cultivate relationships with my known enemies so I can't put it past her. If she did sleep with him it could have resulted from a combination of things, from trying to expose him or her own envy to sheer loneliness and being attention-starved. She tried her hand at online dating, but nothing materialized. She hasn't had a man for as long as I can remember; the only consistent companion she's had is good old "BOB" (battery operated boyfriend). She's had a few of them over the years, from what I understand, she burns them thangs out. To each his own. I keep a couple of them on deck, but I have actual options that are attached to a human being, but for Kairo, that's her only choice.

Even though Kario is my big sister, I've always had to look out for her. Not only did I give her a home for three years, but I also gave her a job. She didn't have what I would call a strong suit or bona fide skill set, but I still found a place for her in one of my various businesses. No matter how many concessions I made, she would always push my patience to the limit. If it wasn't having some sort of challenge with another employee, of growing overly sensitive during a meeting, it was her incessant gossiping. My experiences with Keisha and a few others forced me to implement a policy of not hiring friends and family. But I felt sorry for Kairo, so I put her on the payroll as a receptionist. No matter how I warned her and addressed her inappropriate workplace behavior, time and time again I'd learn that she had been running her mouth, crying on the job, and being where she wasn't supposed to be. I tolerated all that

I could, but when she had a colossal meltdown after spotting Elliot Jr. lurking around my office following our divorce, I had to let her go. The timing of my having to fire her kind of sucked, though, because this coincided with the countdown of her having to move out. I felt a little guilty, but fortunately, Kairo had saved enough money during the time she stayed with me that she was able to step out on her own. I think that her moving on was actually the best thing that could have happened to our relationship.

Her newfound independence seemed to do her some good and my resentment for her behaviors and sloppiness disappeared over time. I may not understand how her brain works or agree with how she handles things, but I will always be grateful for how she had my back during the divorce and the vicious legal battle that was to follow. There were times that Elliot Jr.'s efforts to get under my skin terrorized Kairo. In particular, early one morning she went outside to take out the trash before driving Suga Baby to school and saw Elliot Jr. peel off after leaving something in my driveway. I'm taking a hot shower, bumping Mary Mary's "Go Get It", gearing up to take on another day, when I hear a frantic knock on the bathroom door of my master suite. It was Kario sounding distressed, uttering something about seeing Elliot's custom wrapped vehicle driving away from my home. When I got dressed and came out, she and my housekeeper, Angelita, explained to me that he had left a large bag of Mexican candy on a furniture dolly with a cryptic note. Suga Baby grabbed the note before I had the chance to grab it and instantly had this weird look on her face. This was one of several threats and imposing acts that I would document over the next year. He basically was sending the message that if I didn't comply with his monetary and other demands related to our divorce settlement negotiations that there would be serious ramifications. He signed the note "Cartel Familia" as a way of eluding to his so-called ties to the Mexican Mafia, a claim that he had made throughout our marriage. I had heard him brag about his dealings with the cartel after a few trips to California, but mostly it fell on deaf ears. So, his insinuation that day didn't exactly shake me, but it had Kairo's panties in a bunch. Because she, Angelita and Suga Baby were so disturbed by this, I followed my instincts and made another police report making sure that the incident was on the record. At the time I really only called the police to calm Kairo down and help make Suga feel safe, I had no idea how important keeping a record and making law enforcement aware of his actions against me would be.

There were several other run-ins and suspicious activity that Kario witnessed over the next few months. One time Elliot Jr. stormed into my house through the open garage door, demanding that he be given his antique coin collection and special edition autographed Dallas Cowboys jerseys. Poor Kairo had no idea what he was talking about and from what was told to me, he yelled at her and really cut up, insisting that she contact me and get me to come home. Come to find out I was at the spa at the time getting my bi-weekly luxe facial and massage, and she couldn't get through to me. Apparently, he cursed her out, tore through closets and rummaged in the garage. The sad thing is he clearly hadn't checked the bags and boxes of his shit that I had packed for his ass because everything was in there. I made certain to keep no remnants of him, and give him no reason to return. I get home and find Kairo kneeled in the corner of the living room, overcome with fear and sobbing. I was torn between being livid with Elliot Jr. for having the balls to come to my home acting like a monkey over shit I brought his ass and being irritated with Kairo for losing her composure to this degree. Once again, the local police department got a call and I made a report. After a while, they knew me and my case all too well. I grew resentment for my ex-husband that's hard to describe. The one good thing that came out of the situation is an empathy that I developed for my sister. Later down the line, when the local prosecutor's office decided to file formal first-degree stalking charges against him, I'll never forget how proud I was of her when she faced her fears and took the stand against Elliot Jr. When Kairo testified to all the bullshit he put us through, it tickled me to my soul when she yelled out: "I never slept with you!" It was so funny because the lawyer never even asked her about that. It was like she had been waiting for God knows how long to set the record straight on that rumor. Her outburst was one of many in the courtroom circus that would seal the fate of that no-good gold digger.

"Just a spoonful of sugar
helps the medicine go down."
—Richard Sherman, *Songwriter*

SEVEN

Daddy Issues

SELF-REFLECTION IS A critical aspect of one's growth. Moreover, it's healing and good for the soul. I know what people think when they see me; beautiful, successful, strong, professional, sexy... I'm regarded as an accomplished, educated woman who has her shit together with loads of self-esteem. That's not incorrect. I see myself in this light as well, but admittedly when I look deep within, I have to ask myself what would allow me to fall prey to a gold digger and accept Elliot Jr.'s lack of gratitude and overall bad behavior? What would make me accept and tolerate some of these same qualities in my closest friends, hell even in my very own children? The more I ponder these questions, the more clear to me it becomes.

From a very young age, I witnessed and endured similar toxic patterns and self-serving characteristics in my very own father, Randolph Whitmore Sr. I would describe him as a smooth, well dressed, self-indulging, retired military man. He's very disciplined with a perfect credit score and was a consummate exercise enthusiast. He's older now, in his late 70s, he can't walk, travel, or process things like he used to. It's perhaps his once overactive libido that took the worst blow. After all of his conquests over the past five to six decades, my father finds himself alone fantasizing about women he doesn't have. It took me some time to realize that the ladies he would say he was dating or courting were a figment of his imagination. He would go on and on about this one lady in particular as if she was really a significant love interest. I took to my special cyberstalking skills and tracked the chick down on Facebook. From what I could see, although she was no spring chicken, she was most certainly dating, but it wasn't my father. From what I could tell, she might accept an occasional meal or two, and get a few dollars out of him. She hardly ever spoke to the man and didn't even respond to his texts, I know 'cause I looked through his phone. His current state of being is a bit much to digest, to say the least.

You have to understand, this is a man that for most of my childhood and adult life I have desperately sought approval on some level. Once Sr. got caught cheating on Honey in Germany, my whole life as I knew it blew up in my face. Nothing made sense anymore. The only semblance of a normal, accepting, and loving relationship that I had growing up was with my baby brother Randolph II. He was always special to me, and very much doted on by our parents. As for me, I got so many spankings as a child, I almost became numb. After years of feeling like nobody listened to my cries, I stopped crying out. Expecting my father to show up and rescue his little girl became fruitless. No matter how well I did in school and aspired to achieve, he never acknowledged me or offered the adoration that I longed for, nor the support that I deserved. Even a mere pat on the back or "I'm proud of you" would have gone a long way with me. Sr. did show up at my high school graduation at least. I noticed that he came alone, which was kind of odd because his girlfriend at the time, Natalia, was usually attached to his hip. It wasn't like I missed her or anything, things had been tense between me and her for years. When I was only 14 and would place a call to my father out in California, Natalia would sometimes intercept the calls and use that as an opportunity to bash my mother. This went on for a while, but after a few times, I just told her about herself. I literally let her know that it was completely out of line for her to bad mouth my mother to me. Like where do they do that? She had the nerve to be appalled that I called her out. Instead of having my back, Sr. called himself, checking me for being "too grown for my own good." I didn't give a damn and I made no apologies. Over the years we kept communication to a minimum and agreed to disagree, but I tell you Natalia never said shit else to me about Honey.

Shortly after my graduation as I was getting ready to leave for college, my father asked for my address. I was kind of surprised that he even cared because when it came to helping with tuition, books and other expenses, he literally refused to help me. He told my mother that he didn't feel like I was ready for college and that it would be a waste of his money. I can't begin to tell you how that made me feel, a lesser woman would have broken, but it made me stronger, even more, self-sufficient and determined to succeed. Within a couple of weeks of getting settled in on campus, I received a marriage announcement with a picture of Sr. and Natalia saying that they got married in Las Vegas. It was a slap in my face. It felt like a direct dig to me and to this day, I attribute my father's relationship with her to the reason he wouldn't do anything to help me. Natalia hadn't liked me since I checked her ass back when I was 14.

I love my dad, but our relationship is still strained. As I watch him age and his health deteriorate right in front of my eyes, I can't help but think of how vulnerable he left me to fall prey to a self-serving, arrogant predator like Elliot Jr. I never would have expected things to turn out the way they have because I used to look up to Sr. so much. There was a time when I was in middle school that someone would call, and when I answered, they would just hold the phone, breathe hard, and hang up. This happened off and on for about a month, but one night a man's voice whispered: "I'm watching you." I freaked out and ran into Honey's room to let her hear for herself. The guy didn't say anything, but she heard his breathing. About a week later when we were celebrating Valentine's Day throughout the school with these little hearts and candies called a "Love-Gram," my math teacher sent me one. I truly didn't think anything about it, so when I came home that afternoon, I just left it on the table with my schoolbooks. When my mother came home and saw it signed "Mr. Holt," she hit the roof. She knew I was smart, but I was no mathematician, and there was no reason for my middle school math teacher to be sending me a Love-Gram or showing me any special attention for that matter. All I know is Honey wasn't having it and she made a very rare call to Sr. to let him know what was going on as far as the prank calls and Mr. Holt sending me the Valentine's Day candy. He actually flew into Texas from California to go address the situation at my school. I'm not exactly sure what went down when he and my mother went up to the school, but I was transferred out of Mr. Holt's classroom the next day. For Honey and Sr. to be in the same room, I knew it was serious but just as I was beginning to process his efforts and as him coming to rescue me, my mother thwarted that notion by telling me he had ulterior motives and had been badgering her to let Randolph II come live with him and Natalia out in Long Beach.

A girl's relationship with her father plays a large

role in how she deals with and manages relationships with men. Once I started analyzing the way things played out with Elliot Jr., it occurred to me that I've never had a trusting relationship or dealt with a man whom I could rely on. I guess on some subconscious level I convinced myself to believe that maybe that was too much to ask of somebody. As the saying goes, you can't miss what you never had.

As for Randolph Sr., although I still have respect for him as my father, I don't go out of my way for him just because of the fact that he's getting older. Earlier this year he came to visit me and Suga Baby and to catch a Cowboys vs. Seahawks season playoff game. He's a huge Seattle fan, and I'm a lifetime season ticket holder, so he knows how I get down during football season. It was a long game that went into overtime. Around half time, I started noticing that he didn't seem quite himself. He was particularly quiet, which was unlike him, Sr. was always good for a complaint or some form of criticism of the players, the plays, the peanuts, and hot dogs and especially me. He was dozing off and on during the drive home and didn't have an appetite. When we reached the house, he went straight to bed. The next morning when I got up around 9 am, I realized that he didn't wake up for his 6 am flight back to Cali. When I went into the guest bedroom to check on him, I was immediately assaulted by the stench of piss. My father had clearly urinated on himself. He was lethargic, and I could tell that this was not the first time he had wet himself because he was too comfortable just laying in it.

When Suga Baby and I got him together and to the hospital, he had to be admitted due to complications with pneumonia. He was very sick and couldn't move, but he was talking about needing to pick up his suit from the dry cleaners; that's when I became convinced that the early signs of dementia were setting in. I certainly stepped up to make sure that he received the best care and made him as comfortable as possible in the guest bedroom, but I just couldn't bring myself to go out of my way or cater to him much further than the basics. His weekend visit had turned into a month and as things started to come up, my brother and I realized that one of us needed to go out to his place on the West Coast and make sure things were maintained and taken care of.

After years of sharing his life with Natalia, he now lives alone. She passed away after a series of strokes a couple of years back. I guess I'm supposed to have remorse or feel bad, but she was an awful woman and as far as I'm concerned, ding dong the witch is dead! So now Sr. has to fend for himself, and apparently, he's doing a terrible job at it. On top of his deteriorating health, he's a hoarder. According to my brother, his entire existence is riddled with clutter, he hangs on to everything; papers, mail, take out menus, expired coupons or anything. He hoards clothes, containers and all kinds of crap. The condo looked and smelled like a chemical experiment had gone really wrong. It was so horrible, Randolph II had to have the house cleaned. I'm glad my brother went and dealt with it; there's no way I could have cleaned up his shit after all the years he treated me like shit.

Sr. is mentally going through difficulties, but his doctor wasn't making it any better because his bedside manner sucked. My dad was convinced that he was just a pill mill and not actually treating anything. So, he didn't really want to take prescriptions or any meds, including his blood pressure medicine, so that contributed to what was happening with his fluctuating health. For the longest, he thought he could get his body where it needed to be through exercising as he had for most of his life. In his mind, he could still exercise, but the reality is he's just isn't physically able anymore.

I remember a couple of years back when Suga Baby and I went out to visit. He had signed up to do a 3K run because it culminated with a finish line crossing mixer inside an airplane hangar. For some reason, he really wanted to see the inside of an airplane hangar, but he finished so late that he had to be rerouted since they finally had to close the hangar down. He did finish the run, but by the time he did, nobody was there to see it and they were closing up shop. Needless to say, Sr. didn't get to see inside the hangar. He used to jump out of planes when he was in the military, so I guess that's what all that was about. He was very active back then, bicycling, running, eating healthy, but things had changed drastically. His walk had become a shuffle. When we were in Cali last year and had all gone to Universal City Walk, as Sozey, Suga Baby and I went in and out of stores, Sr. literally stood in the same place for three hours. Eventually, he went on and walked to the restaurant so he'd be there when we got there. He'd be too proud for us to get him a hoveround chair, but he did accept the wheelchair assistance at the airport. Karma and old age are a bitch and, on some level, I think his suffering is direct payback for how he treated me, and specifically my children. His wife Natalia and her daughter, my half-sister Marishia, were Seventh Day Adventists. I was aware of their religious preference, but I didn't know that you weren't supposed to do anything from Friday night till Sunday. So, during a visit many years back when the kids were really young, I was washing clothes, sweeping and tidying up our stuff in their nasty ass house. The kids were watching cartoons and keeping busy with their Game Boys. The next thing I know, Sr. and Natalia had gotten into an argument about the TV being on. I overheard most of the back and forth, Sr. was saying, "She's never here, why should I say something about the damn TV?" The evil witch was on his back, spitting venom, "You know I don't allow the TV on in my house Friday evenings, I don't know who in the hell she thinks she is!" I couldn't believe my ears. He didn't agree with her, but he didn't defend us either. Based on my experience, I knew my father was not about to stand up to her, so for the sake of keeping the peace, I just decided to put an end to this. I pulled him to the side and said, "I'm not here to cause any conflict in your home. I never meant any disrespect; I would never put you in that position. We are going to get dressed and get out of here." He didn't try to convince me to reconsider, he didn't tell Natalia to back off; in fact, for years he upheld her in her bullshit. To this day I feel that my father failed me; he left me vulnerable to be taken advantage of and in jeopardy of weakening my self-esteem. It hadn't occurred to me until I listened to Elliot Jr.'s attorney present his arguments in court, trying to paint a slanted picture of how he was a victim and how I owed him even more of my fortune and that, like my father, he was delusional and a user with no conscience or remorse for failing to provide, protect or stabilize me in any way. If I had let this cycle continue, it would be on me and I would have nobody to blame but myself. I wasn't about to let that happen. And if Elliot Jr. wanted to paint pictures, I was gone bring the biggest brush I could find and stick it right up his ass!

"The truth is sweet like sugar and, lovely like positive moral character to the wise."
—Edward Kofi Louis, *Poet and Self-Made Pen Artist*

EIGHT

Trials and Tribulations

I HAD SET HIM up with a salary, 401K, health insurance, invested in his business and a number of his "get rich quick" schemes, paid his child support, took him and his kids on once in a lifetime trips and even tried to get his life insurance on more than one occasion. During our divorce trial, the issue of whether or not I had a life insurance policy on Elliot Jr. had come up. I testified that I didn't, because he failed a drug test, testing positive for cocaine twice. While I was answering the attorney's questions I smiled inwardly and wanted to burst out laughing when I noticed the interesting look that the stenographer gave him.

That wasn't the only time during our divorce trial when I reflected on what a joke Elliot Jr. really is. I had upgraded him in every fathomable way but if a boy has bitch nigga in their DNA, there's nothing you can do to turn him into a real man. Do you know how embarrassing it was to witness the person I referred to as my husband demand that I pay for his annual Sam's Club card fees? Who does that? Elliot Jr.'s parents must be so ashamed because their only son had no morals and clearly no pride. He even had the audacity to include in his list of demands that I pay for his 24-Hour Fitness membership contract. It hadn't hit me until that moment that I truly spoiled and, to my detriment, fueled his sense of entitlement and lack of self-sufficiency. Elliot Jr. didn't want to have to be responsible for anything to maintain his own damn lifestyle and basic upkeep. He had the mitigated gall to look appalled when the judge directed his attention at me and said; "Mrs. Jennings, go ahead and give him the Sam's card, he's not touching the American Express and if he wants to maintain his figure, he'll have to keep up with his own gym membership." I chuckled and nodded; this shit was in fact laughable. Elliot Jr. and his incompetent attorney had gotten it in their heads that he would go after the luxury cars in my fleet, but I had lawyered up fierce so when it all came down, the only vehicles he was awarded were two cargo vans that I used to transport supplies for one of my businesses and a company wrapped Chrysler 300 which is parked somewhere in need of repairs that he can't afford. Oh yeah, I was also ordered to pay the $600 to have the wrap removed. His pettiness made me detest him.

What could have been a simple severing of ties had turned into a back and forth three-ring circus that took over a year of my time, money and energy. I realized early on that he had ill intentions and came to play a dirty game. So, I made the court aware that he left with things that weren't his, including approximately $30,000 of my personal items including jewelry, clothes, handbags, and other things of value. During cross-examination, his attorney asked me if I like designer bags and if I owned a lot of them. I smugly responded, "I did prior to your client removing them and numerous other personal items from the house." She appeared stunned, his eyes got all bugged, so she quickly moved on. This became the normal dance for her and me throughout the trail. I found that she became easily discombobulated and thrown off, just like her shitty client. She was the perfect reflection of him; like Elliot Jr., she underestimated Sugar Mama and was ill-prepared to face me as an adversary. At one point during the proceedings, "Attorney Incompetent", as I affectionately nicknamed her, complained to the judge that I wasn't answering the questions, and pled with him to instruct me to do so. His Honor retorted, "Mrs. Jennings is answering the questions, just because you don't like the responses doesn't mean she's not complying."

She sat back down flustered. I'm sure there were quite a few moments during the trial when she regretted taking Elliot Jr. on as a client. There wasn't enough money in his account to compensate for the stress of coming up against my legal squad and to pay for the divorce law refresher courses that she clearly needed to enroll in. I was in it to win it, for the simple fact that he had the audacity to sell one of my vehicles behind my back and use the proceeds to hire a divorce attorney and not even talk to me about it. The crazy thing is I don't think he truly thought that his actions, in hiring a divorce attorney, would actually lead to a divorce. It was just a chess move for him...you see, Elliot Jr. is a game player, and when he gets into his feelings, he behaves like a temperamental child. I know that he was just acting out because of the incident that jumped off between him and my son at my place of business a couple of months prior. As far as I'm concerned, all of this mess escalated from that argument that jumped off in my office which ended up turning physical. My initial reaction or lack thereof was more from the perspective that Lil Sozey and Elliot Jr. were both spoiled and a bit dramatic at times. Not to mention, it was late Friday afternoon, I was signing off on outstanding accounts receivable items, and the payroll for over 100 employees and contractors. I was laser-focused on putting out staff-related fires and engrossed in an audit report that Keisha had prepared. Her findings confirmed my suspicions regarding a particular employee's unexplained inconsistencies in billing and slated expenses. So, in the midst of Elliot Jr. and Sozey's fateful squabble, I was up to my ears in corporate minutia. If it wasn't one thing in the life of a mogul, it was another and while the home health care and hospice industries are extremely lucrative, they are equally competitive and there was always someone trying to sabotage my growing empire and take Sugar out of the game on their way to the top.

I was at my desk when I heard Elliot Jr. grumbling about Sozey "talking out the side of his neck", and honestly, I just blew it off. For as long as I could remember, with the exception of a couple of minor disagreements, the two of them got along for the most part. Lil Sozey was seven when I met Elliot Jr., and from then on, they were in one another's lives intermittently based on our dating patterns up until we got married, by that time Sozey was 16, he was working and going to school. Elliot Jr. wasn't a father figure or anything, but Sozey did find a connection with him about the music industry. I'm not sure what Elliot's motivation was, but I know my son had talent and wanted to pursue a career as a recording artist. They were both very interested in the music business so, me being the supportive wife and mother, I sunk about $150,000 into an entertainment company that unfortunately turned out to be another one of Elliot Jr's many defunct ventures. After a series of poorly promoted shows, lackluster mixtape releases, tens of studio hours wasted on drunk and high artists and disagreements between him and Sozey, they simply couldn't get along enough to be productive. Plus, I think Elliot Jr. was jealous of Sozey. He envied his jewelry, designer wardrobe and the cars I bought him. Lil Sozey had acquired my taste for expensive brand names and developed a habit of rocking a new pair of Jordan's every week. This was a typical life for us; he was my firstborn, he was going to school, and doing pretty well so I had no problem lavishing him with these things.

Elliot Jr. had a serious issue with it, though; he used to go on and on about how spoiled Lil Sozey was always telling me that I needed to cut the purse strings. As Sozey got older, he spared no opportunity to tell me, "Sozey isn't as innocent as you think". So that day at my office, I wasn't terribly shocked that they were at odds, but I was completely blindsided when I heard Elliot Jr. yell, "Lil nigga, you ain't shit!" The next thing I know was Sozey spewing, "Naw, nigga, you ain't shit and you ain't never gone be shit without my momma!" Then all hell broke loose. Elliot Jr. leaped from my leather couch then grabbed and choked my son. There was a struggle that created utter chaos in the office, shit was flying off desks. Kairo was crying and screaming as they were tussling in the hallway and knocked frames off the walls. I quickly overcame my shock and yelled at Elliot Jr. to let my son go. Sozey was significantly smaller than him but managed to yank his gold chain off. That seemed to get Elliot's attention more than my voice. Once he snapped out of it, he loosened the grip he had on Sozey, who broke free and stormed out of the office, slamming the glass door into the hallway and throwing the chain on the floor in Elliot Jr.'s direction. People caught wind of the ruckus and were coming out of their offices, whispering and gawking. Worst of all was the white boys looking all red and mortified. I was the owner, the boss and held myself in higher esteem, so this display of ignorance and violence was the epitome of humiliation.

In typical form, my sister Kairo was a complete basket case, hyperventilating at the receptionist station as if she was the one who had been physically attacked. Keisha was gathering up the audit documents and organizing files and papers that had been strewn about in the midst of attempting to calm Elliot Jr. down. I just cut my eyes at them and shook my head in disdain. Admittedly my team was so confused; hell, I was as perplexed as everyone else. As far as I knew, they were getting along. Sozey didn't live with us at the time, but he came over a lot. I wasn't aware of any real conflict, so this came out of the blue. I was pissed, but especially at Elliot Jr., who had retreated into my office huffing and puffing. As the elder, and as my husband, I expected so much more out of him, it was disrespectful on so many levels. As always, Jozette kicked into high gear damage control mode by stabilizing the staff, politely excusing the disturbance and assuring the other tenants that everything was under control.

A few months after he filed for the divorce Elliot Jr. sent flowers to the office, apologizing to my staff for his behavior with a note that read "Sorry, ladies,

I get a little razzle dazzled at times." At that point, there wasn't any reason for me to be moved by that. An apology should have been issued immediately. But nothing could forgive his actions, especially those that would soon follow. I packed up my things to leave so that Elliot Jr. and I could go home and address what had just happened. Sadly, he didn't have anything to say about his action, all he said was Sozey had disrespected him and that he needed to bow down and that I needed to make him do it. That was it, he offered no defense for his behavior nor took any accountability for embarrassing me and violating my place of business. The irony is he felt like he was owed an apology from Sozey. I let him know then and there, "I don't think he owes you shit." That next week we had plans to go to Las Vegas for a business trip immediately following the Cowboys season opener, which I never miss.

During the game, everything seemed to be fine, we ate and drank and cheered "America's Favorite Team" on to victory. During halftime when we went to the bathroom, Elliot Jr. stopped by one of the Cowboys merchandise stalls and racked up a classic Dez Bryant #88 jersey, a bomber jacket, and some other items totaling over $500. When the young lady read his total, he had the nerve to look at me as if I was going to pull out my magic plastic for his ungrateful ass. I rolled my eyes and walked right on to the nachos concession counter and acted like that shit never happened, but he was heated.

As soon as we left the game and got into the truck, Elliot Jr. turned from Dr. Jekyll to Mr. Hyde. He cursed me out in the car all the way to the airport. He went in on me about how much money I blow on Sozey and Suga Baby but treated him like a second class citizen on a budget. He was counting my pockets hard, it was like this nigga had been keeping a tally of all the cars, trips, bags and meals but he spit the most venom on Suga Baby's lavish Sweet 16 extravaganza. Clearly that event had sent him over the brink of envy, and he was bursting at the seams with entitlement and anger. What Elliot Jr. wanted was the ultimate control of the bag. He wanted access to my coin and demanded to be authorized on my business accounts. For a brief stint, right after we first got married, I added him to one of my main checking accounts. I overlooked the radon shopping sprees and unexplained withdrawals every now and again but when Keisha pointed out that the Texas Attorney General could put a lien on my account and joint assets to cover his support payments and arrearage, I was like oh hell naw! Had I left him on my bank accounts, his debt and sheer greed would have no doubt wiped me out or made a serious dent.

We went on to Vegas, as it was already planned and paid for. It was bittersweet for me because Las Vegas had always been a place that we enjoyed together and where we had tied the knot nine years earlier. But something about the way he cursed at me, spoke about my children, attacked my son and had grown increasingly greedy and entitled had taken its toll and I was losing any desire to make the effort to reconcile. If he wanted to restore the peace and bond in the marriage, he'd have to take the initiative and agree to go to counseling on top of that.

Shortly after returning from Vegas, I learned that Elliot Jr. had no intentions of making things better between us; in fact, he had actually set the wheels of a much more sinister plot in motion. It was a Wednesday afternoon, I doubled back from one of my worksites to the house to let in Chai, my interior designer who needed to measure my great room and master bedroom windows for new custom draperies and to grab a pair of sandals for my pedicure appointment. As I opened the door for my designer, the mail carrier was about to put some envelopes in the box. Chai waved and called out, "Would you like me to grab this for you?" I nodded and waved to my mailman. As she and I were in the kitchen talking and going through the fabulous fabric swatches imported in from Paris, I haphazardly flipped through the pile of mail. When I came across an envelope addressed to Mr. Elliot Jennings Jr. from a law office, I really didn't think much of it. Ironically, I rarely ever collect the mail, Kairo usually checks the box on her way in. If I do happen to grab it, it's not unusual for me to open letters addressed to both of us. Elliot Jr. never really got shit other than bills or tickets anyway, so I'd normally just file things away or lay them on the nightstand. But something about this envelope felt off and gave my spirit a little nudge, so I opened it. I discovered that Elliot had paid an advance retainer to a private female divorce attorney with plans for her to file within 30 days of our 10-year anniversary which was less than 3-month outs. This bastard thought he was slick and was getting his ducks in a row to take me for half of what I had worked for and whatever other assets he could come up on. Texas is a community property state, which means that most property acquired during the marriage belongs to both spouses and must be divided in a 50-50 fashion according to the court unless otherwise agreed to otherwise by the divorcing spouses. This means that everything, the homes, cattle, cars, jewelry and the empire that I built all by myself with no help from him would be considered up for grabs in the divorce and would be distributed equally to each spouse. I felt ill. I knew we had not been in a good place for some time, but we were still functioning, still screwing and making plans for the future. It didn't take much for me to realize that all along Elliot Jr. was plotting against me. That was it, Elliot Jr. was a joker who wanted to play, so as far as I was concerned, it was time to let the games begin!

As planned, I went on to Scrub Island, and in between enjoying Mai Tais, sunsets and decadent spa treatments, I filled out the petition for divorce paperwork my attorney had sent me. I faxed everything, paid the $10K flat fee and gave my counsel the go-ahead to file. By the time Elliot Jr. realized that I was on to his ass, it was too late. I had all my shit tight and he had no idea what hit him, his name was removed from everything, I had Jozette change all passwords, logins, and locks on all of my homes and businesses. He had the nerve to try to laugh it off, make light of it and began to backpedal. I wasn't interested in shit he had to say, I merely suggested that he get in touch with that lawyer who he retained to file a petition for a divorce. By the time he did, my attorney had beat her ass to the punch and the proceedings were already underway. There was no turning back; Elliot Jr's days of mooching off Sugar Mama were over and if he thought he was about to cash in this Golden Goose, he was in for the fight of a lifetime. Just like that he went from living in the lavish home he shared with me and mine to sleeping on an old futon in his dusty upholstery shack.

Aside from my bruised ego, I was more irritated about the fact that after I took care of his black ass all that time, he didn't have the human decency to simply talk to me and tell me that he wanted a divorce. If he at least valued the friendship we once had, the relationship could have been salvaged on some level. Had he handled me with some respect and operated with dignity, I would have helped him get set up and on his feet. I never wished ill on him, but now he has me as an arch enemy. Just like all of his failed attempts at anything worth wild Elliot Jr.'s treacherous plan against me blew up in his face. Thanks to the Father above, he was foiled at every turn and ended up looking like an ass. Had he not been exposed, there's no telling what he would have gotten away with and how much more he would have stolen from me. At some point, the court ordered that Elliot Jr. be allowed to enter the home we used to share to gather his belongings and a specific negotiated list of my shit that he had the nerve to squabble over during one of our lengthy and costly mediation sessions, which I had to pay for, of course. I was advised to not be at the property and to allow Mr. Gold Digger full access without interference. It wasn't expressly forbidden for me to have a representative present, so I arranged for Kairo and my ride or die Jozette to let him in and take an inventory of what he took out of the house. It's a good thing that they were there, or Elliot Jr. would have robbed me blind. He had three other people with him, which was excessive considering the amount of stuff he had to get. It became apparent that this was by design to cause a distraction while he ran amuck in my closets. He brought a couple of dudes from the hood and his sister Eugenia, who he knows I can't stand. She is the epitome of hood rat, even Elliot didn't fuck with her like that, so I knew he had stooped to a new low by bringing her along. In fact, the day I met her, they ended up in a heated brawl in their momma's house down in Fairfield. Eugenia was talking reckless, pulled out a knife and actually spit in his direction. The next thing I saw was him snatching her off a barstool and putting her in a chokehold. Her little girl was screaming and pleading for her uncle to let her mama go, their dogs were barking, babies were crying, and Elliot Jr. was foaming at the mouth. Eugenia had dropped the knife but had managed to dig her nails into his arm with one hand while trying to keep her wig in place with her other hand. She had a vicious case of alopecia and was balding in over 80% of her scalp. It was an awful scene. He only let Eugenia go because their mother, Mrs. Jennings, came into the house and went off. She reeked of alcohol and slurred every other word, but her presence seemed to snap them out of it, so he let her go. Then she grabbed her phone and called the police. Elliot Jr. ran out the back door and into the woods.

Mrs. Jennings was pissed at both of them and visibly irritated by my presence. I hadn't gotten any good vibes from her ever, so I'm sure she was not thrilled with the fact that I was seeing all this go down. She was pissed at her son for getting physical with his sister, but even madder at Eugenia for calling the police because Mrs. Jennings had more than her share of run-ins with the law herself and hadn't been home long from serving 18 months in the county for a fourth DUI, this last time was even worse because she was operating her vehicle while intoxicated with her two youngest grandchildren in the car. She had caught two charges for endangering a minor behind having Eugenia's kids in the car while under the influence. Thank God no one was injured when she drove in the wrong direction on a major highway. Needless to say, their family was a mess, and in hindsight, I shouldn't have expected as much decency out of him as I did.

The last time I laid eyes on Eugenia's evil ass was at my annual 4th of July cookout last year. She came to our home apparently trying to show off in front of her stray date. She tried to clown my cooking abilities and accused me of serving store-bought coleslaw and potato salad. When Elliot Jr. noticed the irritated look on my face, he told her to chill out. Eugenia jumped on the defense and started egging on beef between Elliot Jr. and me about him not being the king of the castle. I suggested that she might want to keep it cute in front of company, but she got louder and referred to me as a bitch to her brother. I understand that she had been drinking but I was not about to allow her to disrespect me in my own home. Even though she towered over me at 5'8", I politely slipped out of my Ferragamo wedges, grabbed the long BBQ pitchfork and walked my 5' 1" self right up to her and let her know that if she said another disrespectful word to or about me in my motherfucking home that I would snatch that matted wig off her bald head and toss it on the grill and show her what a real bitch look like. Her date chuckled and Eugenia was fuming, but before she could respond, Elliot Jr. motioned to her date to grab her bag and escorted her out of the house cursing up a storm. I walked out right behind them with the giant fork in my hand. I stood barefoot on my perfectly manicured lawn and dared her to give me a reason for me to exercise my right to bear arms.

Needless to say, when I found out that Elliot Jr.

brought Eugenia with him to collect his things, it burnt my asshole. She went with him all up in my master bedroom and bathroom while the other guys rummaged through the kitchen, pantry, game room and garage. From what Kairo and Jozette were telling me via text and what I could see on my remote camera system, it was sheer chaos. I sent him a text that read; "smile, you're on candid camera :)". I could actually see his reaction when he looked at his phone and read it and then looked up at the ceiling and in the corners trying to spot the hidden cameras. Eugenia was going through my drawers and closets when I was texting him and although I couldn't hear what they were saying, I could see that all of a sudden, they went into the kitchen. When he went back into the room, he was alone filling up black Hefty garbage bags with all kinds of stuff. The two guys went upstairs to get the leather recliners in my theater room and took the framed autographed Cowboy jersey collection off the wall in the game room. While up there, they smoked weed, drank liquor and one of them even took a shit in the commode and left it. That's why I didn't ever want him back in the house. He was supposed to be getting his things and leaving but instead, he and his band of petty bitches defiled my home and stole stuff. Elliot took two of my handbags, he stole a Chanel bracelet, he thought he had the Chanel necklace, but it was a Black House White Market necklace that kind of looked like a Chanel piece. He stole my diamond tennis bracelet, Gucci shoes, Louis Vuitton duffle bag, a Versace bag that he actually brought me one year, with my credit card, several pairs of sneakers and the killer cold Guiseppee crystal-covered shoe boots that Suga Baby wore for her Sweet 16 party.

Most of the things they took can be replaced, but others couldn't because they were one of a kind vintage. Unfortunately, at that time I didn't have any cameras in my closet, only in my hallway and actual bedroom and main living areas. So, the camera didn't capture him or his sister putting my things in his bags so there was no way to tell what he actually took based on what was captured. While on the phone with Jozette, I could hear that he and his crew were so hostile that I was not about to put her and Kairo in any danger by getting into it with them over material possessions. It wasn't that serious, but my attorney was well aware, and God knows the truth. Vengeance is mine saith the Lord, so I knew that he would get what was coming to him and that I would get more things as replacements. I heard that he had sold the items that he was awarded as well as the stuff he stole and has nothing to show and no money to speak of. I've already replaced the stuff they took many times over and I can rest easy knowing that he will never be able to live the life I afforded him, and he is sick about it. I busted my ass and earned everything I have and could do it all over again, Elliot Jr., on the other hand, had done nothing to deserve the fruits of my labor and doesn't have the work ethic or the know-how to get it on his own.

There's no telling exactly how long he had been planning to try to take me for my bag. When I think back on the weeks before I found out that he was planning to file for a divorce, I can recall a number of suspicious moves on his part. Kairo had mentioned him moving papers around in my home office and going through my files. At the time I just assumed he was looking for an ink pen or something or dismissed it as Kairo simply being her overdramatic self. It was later revealed that he had been taking business and banking documents to try to make assessments on just how much I was making. What an ass! The thing is Elliot Jr. and any attorney would have to get up extremely early every day to get even one step ahead of Sugar. They say you don't have to get ready when you stay ready; well, I keep very tight books, and with the help of my bestie Keisha, let's just say I wasn't as vulnerable as he expected.

His 1st attorney requested an over the top laundry list of financial records and documents. Based on the buffoon she discovered Elliot Jr. to be, I assume that she didn't expect me to be able to comply with all of her requests and the established timelines. We were given 60 days to produce the fiscal paperwork, and well within the timeframe all of the records were delivered to her office. I'm certain that she was surprised and overwhelmed. Among the 5,000 plus documents were four years of US tax returns, real estate, business and automobile purchase records and bank statements going back to 2013. There was also an initial temporary court order requiring me to pay him $5,000 a month to cover the "salary" that I had given him, to continue making his child support payments, on top of being responsible for all the mortgages, car notes, the land, insurances, and other bills. I did that for six months until I stopped making the payments to him or for his children. It was ridiculous; by that time his lawyer had dropped him, he wasn't showing up for court or adhering to the mediator, so why should I? It was just a whole bunch of BS that I knew were stall tactics to get my money for a longer period of time. Clearly, I wasn't the only one who saw through his fuckery; two different attorneys decided that they couldn't bother with him, the 2nd attorney gave him his money back.

In the end, our Complex Divorce cost me close to $20K, including my attorney's fees and other expenses. Each time we had to do a deposition or mediation, I had to pay $2,000 to $3,000. When I think about it, this ordeal with Elliot Jr. cost me so much more than just money. He cost me irreplaceable time, energy, some degree of dignity, pride, immeasurable things that have to do with my children and my standing as a professional and most of all my peace of mind during the divorce. I get sick to my stomach when I think about the time I wasted on him because he couldn't be developed. He didn't want to grow in a relationship. He wanted to stay stuck on whatever timeline he was on. As a result, the marriage and the divorce were tension-filled and riddled with Elliot Jr' delaying the process, withholding information, and making outrageous accusations and insane demands.

As the trail was nearing its end, Elliot Jr. would show up for every court day and proceeding, but only because he was thinking that he was going to get something. He had it in his mind that he was going to take me to the cleaners and get half of what I earned and built. After a while, it was embarrassing to watch Elliot Jr. and his attorney going through the motions back and forth about his demands. His own lawyer started to see for herself what a delusional narcissist he is. She eventually realized that he had been feeding her a bunch of lies and staking claim to unverifiable assets, it became clear that he wasn't going to be able to pay her, so she dropped his ass. It was hilarious but tragic at the same time. I just wanted it to be over and he wanted to drag it out as long as he could. When we got ready to go to trial on July 19, 2018, he showed up with a new lawyer, the third one at this point. The judge looked so annoyed but granted him a 30-day continuance. One month later, the judge made the ruling, but our divorce did not become final until three months later on November 3rd because we had to go back to get clarification on the distribution of property.

I can't begin to describe the lesson in humility I had to eat it when it came to conceding certain things that I had acquired during the time we were married. Exhibit B outlined the marital assets and monetary allocation that he would receive. He wanted two of my company cars these cute little Hyundais, so he could give his girls a car each, but instead, he was awarded three company vans. I don't know how the judge came to that, but it was fine with me, I gave him the oldest in my fleet and bought three new ones. The division of cars, cattle, and real estate assets was something that I had prepared myself for. I think it was the petty line items on Exhibit B that irritated the hell out of me. For example, Elliot Jr. literally demanded linens and washcloths. What kind of bitch ass nigger goes after the sheets and towels? The worst part is when he and his sister had emptied my linen closet, he literally only left one towel and one washcloth. I just couldn't believe him; for all those years and for all I've done, and for the simple fact that I bought all the fucking towels, washcloth and linens, how dare he leave me with just one set? I distinctly remember thinking that my life had to be about more than dividing linen. In my opinion, Elliot Jr. had missed the whole boat. If he hadn't reduced us to this, I would've set him up with and furnished for him his own apartment. He didn't have to steal my crock pots, clothes and popcorn popper, we could have gone our own separate ways like mature adults on amicable terms. We didn't have to be friends, but things didn't have to get so messy. At this point, I knew there was nothing for me to say. Mr. Elliot Jennings Jr. had handled me like an enemy, so as far as I was concerned, that's what it was.

During the divorce trial, one of his lawyers was trying to make an argument that Elliot Jr. was an employee of my business, and by establishing this, she felt that it would provide leverage for a greater settlement. Then she went down a path of trying to discredit me by saying that having my husband set up as an employee was illegal. The judge asked, "Was it legal or not counselor? You need to make up your mind. You can't have it both ways". Throughout the proceedings, his lawyer showed her incompetence and lack of preparation for a piece like me on the witness stand. She didn't see me coming. I devoured her like I ate Goldfish crackers for a snack. She was so hot with me, she didn't even say "goodbye" to my attorney, which is highly unprofessional. Clearly, she did not have the trial experience to prevail and hadn't done enough research to keep up. Maybe she had sized me up based on the character of her client if so that clearly proved to be a miscalculation.

She tried to get me on several occasions. Her opening statement began with, "Would you consider yourself a wise businesswoman?" I asked her what her definition of wise is. When she couldn't provide it I said, "Let me help you out, I'm not sure what you call wise, but I can tell you that I am a businesswoman and that's not up for debate." She was trying to make a case but didn't have enough information to build it. I wasn't giving her anything. When Elliot Jr. took the stand, he tried to make the argument that he helped me build my businesses. It was laughable. He might have made a delivery, went to Home Depot or painted a wall a time or two, but there was no proof of a significant or consistent contribution. Worse, he had no information, no witnesses, no documentation or proof whatsoever; other than Jozette, Keisha and Kairo, he couldn't even name any of my other employees nor any other facts about my business. But, how could he? He spent his time getting high and doing whatever he was doing, while I worked 10- and 14-hour days building an empire. Sure, he had his little upholstery business, but his customers were as unreliable and random as he is. We aren't talking about somebody with a steady stream of income.

You might ask, how in his conscience could he make trouble for someone who had given to him so freely? I'll tell you the answer; because he's a gold digger! Elliot Jr. saw me as a lick, a come up and felt like because he laid some pipe that he was entitled to the pipeline. When it was all said and done, Elliot Jr. got about $70K from the sale of one of my properties, close to $400K of my 401K. So, he cleared about $500K liquid but he had to walk away without me, which was priceless.

Overlooking the deep blue Pacific ocean crashing against the cliffs of the Terranea Resort and Spa in Palos Verdes, California, at my "Diva's Divorce" party, my chicas and I raised long-stemmed champagne flutes filled with Ace of Spades and toasted to my freedom. I was deeply thankful that the chapter of my life that included Mr. Gold Digger was finally closed. Little did I know that this was not the end, but only the very beginning of the end.

"She doesn't need your money. Even a penniless fool like you can make her fall in love with you. That's just a miracle."

—Vann Chow, *Shanghai Nobody*

NINE

Mask-a-Raid

I ALWAYS KNEW THAT I had the potential to do and be more than the average. From back in the day when me and Kitty used to tear up these streets, we had our sights on the brothers with a bag. Honey made it plain about what was expected of the men who tried to step to us and, more so, what was expected of me as an independent woman. It was ingrained in me to be a boss; I guess at some point I was either slipping or might just have needed a break from the norm when it came to Lil Sozey's daddy because he was the polar opposite of the ballers I was conditioned or preferred to mess with. I guess there was a disconnect in what had been instilled in me because I know better than to be with a man who has so much less than me. I wasn't all in love with Big Sozey like that, but I was really feeling him at the time. He was from the streets, handsome, laidback and the sex was good. After a while, I realized that he wasn't about nothing, no matter how much I saw in him, he just didn't live up to his full potential. Sometimes I am afraid, maybe even ashamed, to admit that the same may be true with my firstborn. I thought that by me having his son, Big Sozey would make a much better effort to be present and make some legitimate money and contribute in helping to take care of his only child. When Lil Sozey was born, his daddy came around, but it didn't take long for him to fall off. I have no doubt that Sozey loves his namesake, but by the time Lil Sozey was 4, we were totally done. I had had enough of his shit.

Sozey and I haven't talked in years; as far as I'm concerned, he's a lost cause. As for him and Lil Sozey, I was never the type of female to keep a child from having a relationship with their father. He was basically a deadbeat financially, but they did spend some time together, especially when Lil Sozey would go visit his grandmother on the south side of Dallas. She loved him dearly and I could always count on her. She never allowed any of her son's mess to get in the way of her being a supportive and loving grandparent to her only grandson. She is a strong woman of God and I deeply appreciate the way she stepped up and has been a genuine source of love for my son even to this day in his adulthood. In the absence of a viable daddy or co-parent, I had to step up and do whatever it took to be there for my child. Although I knew that it wasn't my fault, deep down I felt bad that Lil Sozey's father was absent from much of his life. I saw the disappointed look on his face when Big Sozey failed to come through or broke yet another promise to pick him up or show up to a special activity at his school. I knew the feeling of thinking your father didn't care or made other things or people a priority so I was determined that my child would be insulated as much as possible from those emotions. In hindsight, I realize that this is where my habit of overcompensating or placating him with gifts of clothes, new sneakers every week, jewelry, video games and all kinds of materialistic possessions to fill that void came into play. By the time he got into his early twenties, shit started to spiral out of control and his sense of entitlement was not only off the Richter Scale, but it was also downright scandalous. The truth is, I had created yet another monster, except this spoiled brat was my own flesh and blood. At some point toward the end of my marriage to Elliot Jr., it became painfully obvious to me that not only did I need to regain control over my spending and spoiling of him, but that I needed to pull back significantly with Lil Sozey. For as long as I can remember, Elliot kept badgering me about setting limits when it came to what I did for my son, but I just couldn't react to or receive that advice coming from a gold digger. I knew how jealous he was of Sozey because he had access to money, the stores where I maintained accounts, professional sporting team tickets, and my cars. That boy has wrecked a Mercedes 350 Sedan and a new Silverado pickup truck. One of my Hyundai work cars and an Impala with rims that he loved ended up in the impound. As for the latter, the agreement was that he would pay the car note, and I would take care of the insurance, but Lil Sozey's ass never honored that at all. That car had been impounded so many times for his negligence in maintaining the tags and registration that I was over it. I would have left it in there, but his grandmother was gracious enough to co-sign for that vehicle, and his behavior was beginning to affect her credit. I had too much love and respect for her to let it go down like that, so month after month I paid the damn car note for him and made sure the coverage was current. Lil Sozey never seemed to have the same consideration; every time I bailed him out of a situation, he would say all the right things at first and fake like he was on the right path.

Then the next time I looked up, he was on some more BS or posting pictures and videos of him drinking, smoking and acting recklessly on social media. At times all I could do was shake my head. I truly had high hopes Sozey to make a life for himself. My son is educated, courtesy of a four-year college program funded by yours truly. He earned a bachelor's degree in Business Administration and is extremely talented in music and very charismatic like his mother. I could never understand why Sozey won't just focus and become self-sufficient. In spite of his schooling and my example as a serial entrepreneur, he wants to be a hustler and always finds himself back on the streets. As much as I hate it, I understand why Sozey is so drawn to the fast life and the hood. Still, there's no excuse for his irresponsible and self-serving behavior and sometimes he seems oblivious to all that I've done for him and thinks that because I brought him into this world, I have to finance his experience in it.

I invested all that money in Elliot Jr.'s now-defunct entertainment company not to merely pacify his whims, but in the hopes that Sozey's music career would pop off or that he might at least stumble on a passion that would be constructive for him. Even after they parted ways on that venture, Sozey convinced me that pursuing a rap career was going to keep him out of trouble and that he was ready to focus and take it seriously. I went all-in for my son, I hired him a full-time publicist, financed several music videos, flew him to Los Angeles to shoot an EPK, set him up in a house out there, booked studio sessions, artist development, a choreographer, personal trainer and a chef! I spared no expense in dropping a bag on my client/son. If Sozey wanted a track from a particular producer, a feature from a popular artist or a videographer to follow his every move for social media content, I made it happen. I brought on a number of experts so as I would get positive feedback, or see tangible results or deliverables, and

I would feel validated, but I began to realize that the more I did for him, the more he expected and took me for granted. When his PR team would book an event for him to attend or when it was time to shoot a video, in addition to travel or production costs, he would show up to my office, wreaking of weed, demanding thousands of dollars for wardrobe. It got to the point that he didn't even bother asking me for money for clothes anymore, he would go to the mall to the stores and boutiques where I have accounts or cards on file and rack up outrageous tabs for designer outfits. I tried to justify his expenditures as business expenses and potential write-offs, but it didn't take long for me to discover that my son/client had lost his natural-born sense.

I reached my ultimate limit when he charged $4,000 worth of clothes on my store accounts to wear to my 50th birthday events in New Orleans. I mean who does that? What made my son feel justified in picking, pulling and ringing up designer slacks, jackets, tops, shorts, and shoes on my dime, to attend a celebration for me? Even if I had said go ahead and get you an outfit, I would think that he had the sense and decorum to keep it at that. But no, he balled out on Rockstar, Gucci and some other Italian designers. The crazy thing is I never even saw the outfits during my B-Day festivities in the Big Easy.

On the Friday morning of the welcome mixer at one of the most fly hotels in the French Quarters, I get a random call from Sozey sounding annoyed and frustrated. Instead of being on the highway to New Orleans like I assumed, he was at my house in Dallas asking the whereabouts of the keys to my Porsche Panamera. Here I am getting the glam treatment from my squad, flown in from all over the country, and Sozey is giving me some lame story about his car getting impounded again and how I need to quit tripping and come up off the keys to my car so he can get on the road. After everything that happened and with Sozey's track record, I couldn't let him use my car and take the chance of him wrecking it.

When we got off the phone I just figured that he would borrow one of his female friend's cars, ride with a homie or maybe even fly down, if not that for the meet and greet that night, but at least in time for the parade on Saturday leading up to my actual party. Before I knew it, I was consumed with getting my makeup done by my go-to artist Mikell, the first of four custom lace front wigs installed by my day one stylist Tia, who was going through my looks and accessories with my wardrobe stylist Bella. Suga Baby and her boyfriend kept checking on me and giving me updates about the various family members and friends who were arriving in the hotel. Jozette and the rest of my team were taking care of last-minute celebration details, checking in guests and executing our flawless event plan. In addition to my staff from Dallas, I hired a local New Orleans party planner, a decor specialist and a florist to help transform the House of Blues Foundation Room into a magical masquerade ball and pop up concert. No expense was spared or stone left unturned with my "Fabulous 50th" destination extravaganza. I had so much to celebrate and was honored that so many people had converged on one of my favorite cities. More than anything I felt grateful to be in the position to throw a three-day event of this caliber.

In addition, to decadent food spreads, flowing liquor, live entertainment, and non-stop activity, each guest was laced with a "Keilanii's Fabulous 50th New Orleans Survival Kit" that included customized candles and potato chip bags, hangover supplies, a bottle of wine, Mardi Gras beads, hangover medicine, and the city's infamous caramel pralines. Even though I felt like I was on top of the world, I couldn't escape this nagging feeling that something wasn't quite right. There was so much going on that I just tried to shake it off, but Suga Baby could sense it and so could Baby Boy. A couple of times I found myself looking out the window or opening the door of my room and looking down the hallway. My personal paparazzi followed everyone all weekend and captured some wonderful moments, but I kept getting this weird feeling that someone was watching me. It was just a heaviness in the air, and I kept catching a whiff of a bad smell that put me in the mind of Raid bug spray. Even now when I think of it the hair on the back of my neck stands up. Whenever the thought would come to mind, I'd just dismiss it, or take a shot of cognac, champagne or whatever was nearby.

After a while, it occurred to me that between everyone posting our every move on social media feeds and all the people moving shoulder to shoulder on Bourbon Street that I was being paranoid. So, I threw back another shot and got my party on.

I woke up early Saturday morning a bit exhausted. I had tossed and turned all night, so I was happy to be headed out to grab a coffee and some beignets; see, you can't go to the NOLA and not eat beignets. Baby Boy was still knocked out so I was meeting a couple of my girls who flew in from LA in the lobby so we could grab a car over to Cafe du Monde. When I opened the door I almost stepped right on top of a medium-sized box with a ribbon tied in a bow. I just assumed it was another birthday gift so I popped it under my arm, and with my small Gucci tote on my left wrist and my iPhone in my other, I proceeded to the elevator texting my girls. On the quick ride down to the lobby, I shook the box but didn't think much of it. Once I reached the busy reception area, my phone started pinging with responses; as usual, I was always the first to arrive. Kitty was laid up with her man of the moment so she wasn't coming. Kairo was running around with like a chicken with her head cut off trying to find her glasses and room key and said she was coming down as soon as possible. Shiloh, who works in my Branding and Marketing department, was minutes away and Skylar on my Communications team was in the gift shop. Normally Keisha would have been there, but lately, she had been on some bullshit. I had to let her go as far as working with me due to some inconsistencies and a few questionable moves, but there was no hardcore evidence of actual wrongdoing so as far as our working relationship I had to put some distance between us. To me, she was like family, so in spite of the professional aspect of things, I didn't see any cause for us not to deal with one another. I'm not so sure she felt the same, especially since the divorce. Elliot Jr. had made several sly remarks hinting that someone I thought was my friend was giving him intel. I could never prove it was Keisha, but from that time since, the vibes she was giving off were weird. It was like she couldn't look me in the eye. I hadn't seen her in three to four months until she popped up my office the week before we headed out for Louisiana and dropped off a birthday card with ten crisp $100 bills. It was appreciated, but super odd to say the least. She said it was her way of making things up to me, I wasn't exactly sure what things she was referring to, but I said: "Whatever, K, it is what it is." She let me know that she had received my custom broach clasped, French silk-covered "Fabulous 50th" invitation, but that she wouldn't be able to make any of my events. It would be the first birthday we didn't celebrate together in some way since we were 21, but at this point, nothing surprised me about her. When everyone finally got to the lobby, we were all laughing and sharing stories about the night before, and I had almost forgotten about my gift. Skylar was the one who reminded me, asking all excitedly "Oooo wee what do we have here?!" motioning toward the box under my arm. Everyone was all giddy and hyped looking on as Shiloh offered to hold my bag while I undid the intricate bow. For a minute, we were all in awe and silent when I took out this creepy doll made out of burlap, sticks and felt, dressed in a replica of a wool Chanel suit with a handbag, that, I dare say, resembled me. Kairo is the one who snapped us out of it when she started crying and screaming, all buck-eyed behind her horn-rimmed glasses, "Oh no! Keilanii, that's a Voodoo doll!" I dropped the box and was about to throw the damn doll when Skylar touched my hand and said calmly but firmly, "Listen to me, do not panic, many people, especially here in New Orleans, practice and believe in Black Magic, so this is not to be taken lightly. This is a blatant threat and intended attack on you, but the God we serve will not have it!"

At this point, we all moved to a seating area off of the main lobby. For the first time in a long time, I was almost on the brink of tears. My head was spinning, and that Raid smell was still permeating my nose and throat. Up to that point, I couldn't fathom where that smell was coming from. I realized that whoever was responsible for this doll was fooling around with Voodoo. Causing people to feel sick or be plagued by the smell of bug spray was a tell-tell sign of that. Skyla insisted that we all pray. I sat the doll down in the box on the coffee table in between us and we bowed our heads, held hands and began to give God the glory, to ask for guidance, clarity, and protection. As we came out of it, I felt a sense of peace and noticed that Suga Baby and several other friends and family members were approaching us. I didn't want to get anyone else upset or drawn into this situation, so I gave my daughter my credit card and instructed her to go into the hotel's coffee shop and order beignets and coffee for everyone. I assured her that we would be there shortly. Once they walked off, Shiloh looked up from her phone and explained, that based on her experience and Google search that there is a proper way to dispose of a Voodoo doll and that one should never just throw it away or burn it under any circumstances. She said that this will release bad energies, entities, and spirits attached to it and that they will latch on to me, possibly forever. She explained that the doll had to be sent away from me and that we had to wrap it in a white cloth for purification and light energy cleansing and throw it into a river or stream where it can be carried away by the water farther and farther away from me. She was adamant that once I toss it, I must turn away and leave and not look back. We agreed not to speak of this or involve anyone else. Kitty was a nervous wreck; and as much as I wanted to leave her behind at the hotel while we went to deal with this, I knew that she could not hold water and I didn't want her upsetting any of my other guests or further dampen the vibe of my festivities. So, after greeting everyone who had made their way in the coffee shop, we took our cups and baked goods to go.

After stopping in a few shops on Canal Street, I found some white cloth and we walked over toward the popular Outlet Collection at Riverwalk. The small mall is located along the Mississippi River waterfront, so it was easy for us to access it. We all stood together, Skylar said a few words of prayer, I wrapped the doll and dropped it into the river. We immediately turned and walked, better yet ran away, never to look back.

Once I reached my suite, it was time for my glam squad to arrive. Jozette was giving me a rundown of pertinent details, and Baby Boy was ordering room service. As Mikell was setting up his station and Bella was buzzing and going on and on about how I was going to shut down the whole French Quarter, I was slowly starting to feel a bit more at ease. I had Jozette pour me a mimosa and asked if my son had arrived yet. She double-checked her list, called down to the front desk and they confirmed that he had not checked into his room. I was admittedly irritated but dismissed those thoughts once my food arrived. The smell that was troubling me had gone away and my appetite was really kicking in.

Over the next hour and a half, Tia transformed my hair into a flowing ombre unit colored in pink, aqua and gold. I was poured into a Swarovski crystal-covered bodysuit accented with iridescent, Gucci, thick-soled sneakers and a jewel and feather-adorned parasol. I felt like a superstar as my entourage and I made our way through the lobby and onto the grand staircase of the hotel that spilled onto Bourbon Street. The looks on the faces of my loved ones, respected colleagues, and passers-by were electric; it was like I could see myself shining in their eyes and reflecting on the brass instruments of the jazz band. And just like that, led by the Zulu Tramps I floated at the head of a sea of masked people, dressed to the nines, through the streets of the French Quarter. As the horns were blaring, I strutted my stuff celebrating my life, not caring who was staring. The energy was amazing, the music was intoxicating, and love was undeniable. It was almost surreal like I was in a dream and just like that it wasn't anymore.

We arrived at the House of Blues, where my official party was taking place; everyone was so joyous, smiling, dancing, taking pictures and basking in the exhilaration of the parade experience. I was about to go in and change into my jaw-dropping birthday outfit when my 85-year old auntie who had traveled all the way from South Carolina asked to take a picture with me and the Zulu Tramps; she was fascinated with their painted faces and tribal costumes. As they were helping her out of the bicycle chariot that Jozette had arranged for her to be transported in the parade in, I noticed someone, a man, moving in and out of the crowd. Like most of my guests, he was wearing a mask and seemed oddly familiar. By this time my auntie and I were standing side by side with the large entertainers on either side of us. The paparazzi were in full force and many onlookers were even recording and taking photos. Kitty took our aunties and yelled for us to say "Cheeeese!" As my teeth were clenched for the pose, my eyes caught a glimpse of the man again, this time he had removed his mask. From a distance with what seemed like a thousand bodies between us, our eyes met. My stomach dropped and my nostrils filled with Raid.

Sozey never showed up to New Orleans. In fact, I didn't hear from him for a few months after he blew off my 50th. He never apologized and acted like nothing had ever happened. He even had the nerve to wear all the expensive clothes he'd bought on my account in a music video he posted online. When Baby Boy pointed it out to me, it stung a bit, but Sozey couldn't hurt me anymore. That would be the last shopping spree he would ever enjoy at my expense. The sad thing is, he probably doesn't even realize that him not showing up for an occasion that meant so much to me changed something deep inside me and it altered that way I see us. He is my son and I will always love him, but he'd made it quite apparent where he stands with me, so that makes it easier for me to handle him accordingly. At this juncture in my life, I welcome boundaries and clarity and I no longer feel obligated to people based on blood or history. As for my "Fabulous 50th", when the masks came off, I came to accept that the people who were there were supposed to be there, all except for one.

"The world is made of sugar and dirt."

—Alfred Döblin, *German-Jewish novelist*

TEN

When the Tables Start to Turn

My "Fabulous 50th" in New Orleans was, without question, one of the best times I've ever had, and I'm sure all of my guests felt the same way. The love and accolades poured from near and far. I was still on a high, basking in the energy of the festivities and looking at all of the posts on social media on my iPhone while I was waiting in the Starbucks drive-through. I was scrolling the Gram waiting on my Grande Caramel Macchiato with extra whipped cream when my bliss was interrupted by calls and texts from Jozette, Kairo, and several other people from my headquarters. I was thinking "What in the hell?" I collected my coffee and a buttery croissant and proceeded down the road, making my way to the highway in the direction of my office, which was literally only a few minutes away. I dialed Jozette back using the Bluetooth in my white Panamera. When she answered, I sensed that she was not her usual calm and collected self. I also could hear a commotion in the background. Jozette asked if I was okay and where I was. I told her I was pulling off the exit and about to turn into the complex where my office was located. She told me to be alert and proceed with caution, explaining that Elliot Jr. was in or around our building. She told me that two staff members came in and informed her that they believe they saw him lurking in the parking lot, but that Kairo set off the pandemonium when she came barreling in the office screaming and crying after spotting him the parking lot in a dark blue vehicle. According to Jozette, they damn near had to call the paramedics to stabilize her from hyperventilating.

At this point, I'm pulling into the structure, parking in my reserved spot, so I told her that I would be inside shortly. She insisted on coming down to help me with my things, but I assured her that I was fine. So many crazy thoughts were racing through my mind as I was collecting all of my stuff. I quickly shook it off, and instead focused on balancing my coffee, an extra pair of comfortable shoes, my Birkin bag, files, and car keys. After activating my alarm and scanning the parking lot, I made my way across the road in between the parking structure and the glass doors of my office lobby. Out of nowhere, I felt chills race up my body, so I picked up the pace. I looked to the left then to my right and caught a glimpse of a dark vehicle with tinted windows creeping around the corner. Rather than heading toward the doors, for some reason, I immediately spun around on my heels and was frozen in place. The vehicle sped up to the stop sign right at the walkway and rolled down its passenger window just enough for me to see the driver, who was wearing a camouflage jacket. It was Elliot Jr.; he had on dark glasses and was holding a Glock with his right hand that was resting on his lap. Just as he lowered his frames and we made eye contact the same way we had two days prior in the French Quarters, Jozette placed her hand on my shoulder and grabbed my arm, pulling me in the building. Elliot Jr. sped off and I snapped out of it. Sugar is rarely ever knocked off her square, but for that brief elevator ride, I had to fight back my emotions and the fear that I had been suppressing for months. I had planned to make a beeline for my office suite in the back and wrap my brain around everything that had just transpired, but no such luck for me.

My big sister had turned my reception area into a three-ring circus. There was one person fanning her with a folder, another one was rubbing her back proclaiming, "The devil is a liar," and my new accountant Jon was bringing her bottled water. I was glad that Kairo was in one piece, but I instantly regretted giving into her pleas for me to let her come back to work part-time. This display of drama was precisely what I found to be unacceptable workplace behavior, so on top of my nerves being rattled, Kairo had me pissed. The non-stop ringing of the phones was the last straw, I spazzed out yelling, "Why is no one answering the phones? If you value your job here, then I suggest everyone get back to work; if you want to cater to Kairo, then you can all pack your things and go elsewhere, and that goes for you too Kairo!" I stormed through the office and started putting my things away and settling in. I was determined to get back on track and not let Elliot Jr. throw me off my mark. His presence and antics had already sidetracked much of our morning.

After about 20 minutes, Jozette knocked on my door, and when she came in, I asked her to shut the door behind her. She let me know that everyone was back to normal and that Kairo had calmed down considerably. Come to find out, Elliot Jr. followed her into the parking structure, up to the second level where she normally parks, and blocked in her vehicle. Not recognizing the car, she got out to demand that the driver tell her what was going on. She was stopped in her tracks when she realized that it was Elliot Jr., who had rolled the window down and pointed the gun right in her direction. Kairo felt faint but then went into a state of panic yelling, "Help!" at the top of her lungs. She was looking all around, hoping for someone to assist her, and then Elliot Jr. drove off. Jon was running toward her asking what was going on and if she was okay. As he helped her across the walkway, he confirmed that he had seen him as well, head on through the windshield while he was headed in Kairo's direction. This was so irritating and mind-boggling. What did he want? What was he trying to prove? What would he do next? First was the Mexican candy stunt with the morbid note, the degrading social media posts, and the cryptic text messages. Then it progressed to late-night phone calls, sightings in my neighborhood and showing up unannounced at mutual acquaintance houses. I thought that it couldn't get any worse than being stalked during my birthday parade or being the victim of Black Magic, which came with the night sweats, loss of appetite, and the lingering putrid smell of Raid and the Voodoo doll. Now Elliot Jr. had gotten brazen enough to drive down on me and my loved ones and staff brandishing a firearm. This was getting out of control and progressively worse. It became clear to me at that moment that up to this point, I hadn't taken his actions and threats as seriously as they actually were. I had no choice but to contact the police, but this time would be different than the various reports I had made over the past year. This time I was actually scared. This time I had witnesses. This time he had me shook.

Because my office was in Dallas, I had to file a report of the incident there. Other than the shit he pulled in New Orleans, all of the other incidents had taken place within the jurisdiction of the town I lived in, so I had made all of the reports to the local Rockwall County Police Department. A Rockwall

County detective was assigned to the case, but other than receiving a voice message from her a few weeks back assuring me that she was looking into my case, I didn't heard anything else. To be honest, I had been so consumed with preparing for my party and getting to the bottom of identifying the disloyal snakes within my organization that it never even crossed my mind again. Now things were different; Elliot Jr. was getting bolder by the day and reckless with his threats.

Every week I'd get a series of crazy messages that ranged from him threatening me and my brother to him asking for some pussy. I was baffled, I couldn't for the life of me understand what his aim was in going to these extremes. He got the sheets, the clothes, a couple of cars, cows, a bankroll, and a fucking Sam's Club card. What more did he want? I'll tell you what; Elliot Jr. had a killer sweet tooth and his craving for Sugar had him going crazy. See, as I suspected that gold digger had gotten caught up on the lavish lifestyle, but he was sprung on Sugar! Between the handstands, tongue tricks and squirt sessions, I had Elliot Jr. hooked, and no judge's orders or divorce decree could alter his deep desire for me. What made it even worse was his seething anger in knowing that I had moved on to his nephew Ross. He hated that I was fucking around with Ross. The thought of me turning out Baby Boy sexually like I had done him had clearly driven Elliot Jennings Jr. to the brink of insanity.

His obsession, fueled by jealousy, had sparked

a series of drive-bys, text messages, emails, and voicemails. Out of nowhere, I started getting calls and messages on my phone from CheerStar Athletics, the gym where Suga Baby had been a member of their champion competition cheer team for many years. When I returned the coach's and owner's calls, I was able to get her head coach on the line. She sounded disturbed and genuinely concerned about my daughter's safety. Apparently, Elliot Jr. had stooped so low as to contact Suga Baby's cheer squad to try to defame her reputation, in an effort to get under my skin. In his bullshit voicemail, he had the nerve to say that he was merely calling out of concern for the other kids on the team. He went on to ask them how they could justify having a murderer on the cheer squad and if they knew that she was the getaway driver in an assassination of a Latino man. I was heated as I listened to her coach detail the voice message. The coach went on to assure me that she and everyone at CheerStar Athletics had come to know me and Suga Baby and, moreover, her character for the past six years and that they had no doubt that his call was baseless. However, they were on high alert for Suga Baby and all of the participants of their organization. Elliot Jr.'s rants were the equivalent of a "madman" as she described and confessed that his creepy voice gave her eerie goosebumps.

Those folks out in these affluent communities and suburbs that CheerStar caters to don't play games when it came to safety and took all threats as serious.

I advised them to report his calls to the police and assured them that I was doing the same thing and asked that they save the recordings. Everything Elliot Jr. did backfired in his face. I guess he thought that he was invincible, or that there wouldn't be any consequence for his actions. On some level, I think he felt like he didn't get enough out of my pockets from the divorce. On another level, based on his own words in messages and texts to me, he felt that I had taken things too far and that he never really wanted to actually break up with me. I can't explain his actions or what pushed him to the point of extreme unwanted pursuit, but what started off in my mind as just stupid games had progressed into bona fide stalking. Now on top of everything else I had to deal with fear and concern for my safety and for people that I care about.

At some point, Elliot Jr. had to realize that it was game over when Texas Marshals arrested him at his upholstery shack and charged his ass with violating Texas Penal Code 42.072, Third-degree felony stalking. Based on all of the reported incidents, his social media posts, the drive-by outside my office and the phone calls to CheerStar Athletics, the Rockwall County Prosecutor's Office made the decision to pursue the case against him. According to Texas law, stalking is classified as conduct where the actor commits an offense that the other person will regard as threatening, such as bodily injury or death for the victim or member of their family. It also includes giving the victim reason to believe that they or their property are in danger or to make them feel harassed, annoyed, alarmed abused, tormented, embarrassed or offended. Shit, there was no wonder why they threw the book at Elliot Jr. They couldn't punish him for being a gold digger, but they could get him for the deep ass hole that he had dug for himself by stalking me. The charge could garner a sentence of imprisonment for 5 to 99 years or life and up to $10,000 in fines.

I could only imagine what was going through his head when he was being booked, searched and locked in that cold cell. Was he so delusional or narcissistic to believe that there would be no consequence to his actions? I wondered if he talked to anyone about the situation, his actions or what he was now facing. Who advised this clown? Who did did he confide in? I met his family and I knew their toxic dynamic so I doubted very seriously that he would really tell them the truth. Throughout our entire acquaintance and subsequent marriage, he was always too prideful to let his relatives or anyone in his circle in on any problems he was facing. His pride was too strong, and he loved to keep up appearances, especially when it came to his immediate family. He and his sister were almost always at odds and had a very unhealthy sibling rivalry. His alcoholic mother, even in spite of her own legal troubles, had the nerve to stay up on her hind legs and was super judgmental. But worst of all was The Chief. OMG, Chief Jennings was by far one of the most critical, self-absorbed and hard to please men I have ever met. I knew there was no way Elliot Jr. was keeping it one hundred with his father. He always felt inferior to his daddy and worried that he never could live up to his expectations. I'm sure that Elliot Jr. flaunted me and all the bells and whistles that came along with marrying me as a means to showboat for his father's approval. If anything, I believe it made him think even less of his son. See The Chief is one of these supposed men of valor who stands for honor and integrity. When it came to the seed of his loin, however, those traits must have skipped a generation because neither Elliot Jr. nor Eugenia exhibited any honorable character whatsoever.

During our marriage, I had no problem with his father; in fact, I found him to be the most reasonable and tolerable person in their entire fucked up clan. What little respect I held for The Chief had been lost when he called me being nosey about Suga Baby when that trouble had first jumped off. On top of that, when it came to our divorce, The Chief had made no apologies in upholding his son in his gold digger mentality and encouraged him to take me for every penny he could. I have to admit that I was a bit taken aback by his position although I shouldn't have been. He preached honor, but I've had my doubts about where he truly stands. Some men will go to great lengths to perpetuate a facade and even convince themselves that their own bullshit is true. Some years back I was privy to a heated conversation between Elliot Jr. and his mother while she was in prison for the DUI and reckless endangerment of a minor charge. During one of the many collect calls or pre-paid calls that I foot the bill for, she was going off about how The Chief was a hypocrite and that he didn't want her to expose him, blowdown his house of cards, or knock him off his "purple pedestal". When I asked Elliot Jr. about it, he explained that for many years there had been a hush-hush rumor in the family that Elliot Sr. had acquired his U.S. Military Purple Heart fraudulently. It was no secret that his daddy came from a military family, and before he became the Chief of the Fairfield Fire Department, which is how he was nicknamed "The Chief", Elliot Sr. had served in the United States Air Force for a short time. Being that my father too was a career military veteran, I had some insight into these things. It always struck me as odd that after serving only one year, Elliot Jennings Sr. was awarded the Purple Heart, which is the highest honor that can be bestowed for a courageous act. Now, mind you, every Purple Heart recipient has a story that comes along with it, and although not everyone shares their experience, The Chief has a boastful and boisterous personality and prides himself in being the family's, community's and local fire department's unofficial historian. He was given an Honorable Discharge and a full military benefits package, yet to this day, no one has heard the story of how the highly esteemed accolade came to be. I fought hard to keep my eyebrows down when

I learned his brother worked in the United States Military Honor Division where they issue special accreditations and distinctions. I don't have any proof of these speculations, but I know that if The Chief or his black-ass son rightfully has any piece of a heart, it damn sure ain't purple.

Now Elliot Jr. was sitting in a cold jail cell, forced to face his demons and the consequences of his actions and I wondered if his own family would have his back or fuel his tendency to project and deflect. Knowing that he had been detained brought up mixed feelings. It may seem that the obvious reaction would be for me to celebrate, or bask in Elliot Jr.'s misery, but to be honest I felt angry and frustrated. I wanted this to be over! I had wasted the last nine years of my life, hell, technically far more than that, on a man who lied, violated and took advantage of me. I could have been bitter purely based on the fact that he came for my bag. I could have hated him for stealing my belongings and wished him dead for attacking my son, posting Suga Baby's mugshot and accusing her of being a snitch, getaway driver and calling her a murderer in the message to CheerStar Athletics. At this point, I just wanted to not have to hear his name, respond to his antics, give the side-eye to close friends who he claims to have slept with, wonder if Baby Boy was planning on using his advice to eat greedy or deal with anything that has to do with him. I had tried to do everything in my power to move on and reset my life. Yet despite the fact that I wasn't doing anything to intentionally provoke him, his obsession for me, or maybe it was the lifestyle that I provided for him, had sent him over the edge. That coupled with an overinflated ego drove him to seek an audience and cross boundaries that now had his very freedom in jeopardy. My how the tables had turned.

"Don't worry about a sugar planter. Give him a horse and he'll ride to his own funeral."

—Curtis Siodmak, *German screenwriter*

ELEVEN

The State Of Texas Vs. Elliot "Gold Digger" Jennings

"HAVE YOU EVER had your name on the other side of a vs. and the name that your name was opposing was the State of Texas or the United States of America?" We all watched in awe as Elliot Jr. spoke brazenly into his phone's camera for one of his live social media rants. That video that hard garnered about 357 views online had now made its way into the Rockwall County, Texas Courthouse, entered into evidence as Exhibit 1 by the State's Attorney Bradley Ratcliff. The Honorable Judge Henley Atkinson had allowed the video to be published on the courtroom's digital overhead projector. Elliot Jr. continued with his madness, "I ain't never been the choochie type nigga to even fuck with social media, but I feel like my life needs to be a testimony for some of you coochieroni type motherfuckers, some of you tender-dick niggas... man, I feel like I'm in the fight of my life, but like The Chief says, 'When you a child of God, what can they do wit' you?' Everyone in the courtroom looked on attentively, trying to make sense of what was being played and the message that Elliot Jr. was trying to convey when he recorded the post. He appeared to be parked in a vehicle somewhere with the overhead light on. It was dark outside, Houston rapper Pimp C's "Long Live the Pimp" was playing in the background as he continued his message. "Imma tell you the real-life story of a real motherfucker who went against all odds, the State of Texas, District Attorney of Dallas and a real-life fucked up bitch! Imma use this platform that motherfuckers tried to destroy me on, assassinate my character, but I don't want to get too deep into no intelligent shit cause I don't want them motherfuckers to overrate me but I will use it to expose these mother fuckers that's weaker than wet toilet paper."

While the video was playing, I sort of tuned out and began to analyze everyone who was present. On the prosecution's side sat my family, friends and a couple of close colleagues, including Shiloh and Skylar, as well as various detectives, law clerks, prosecutor's office employees and some folks I didn't recognize. The folks on the defense side looked like the cast of the UniverSoul Circus. The pew style seats were occupied by his immediate family. Eugenia, true to form, wore a cheap wig that rose up in the back revealing a gap between her neck and the wig. The exposed hair on the nape of her neck was knotted in tight little balls like an old man's chest hairs or taco meat, it was disgusting. Elliot's parents were seated in the first row, in front of Eugenia. Their mother had aged considerably since the last time I had seen her. Cleary all those years of alcohol abuse had taken its toll because her black had certainly cracked. She wore a two-piece, chartreuse green knit pantsuit and some leopard printed closed toe wedges. Even Elliot Jr.'s once statuesque father seemed to have shrunk over the past couple of years. The prideful former Fire Chief was hunched over and appeared weary or thoroughly embarrassed by his namesake. He wore a simple charcoal argyle sweater, black slacks and dark sunglasses inside the bright courtroom. There was Chuck, one of Elliot's drinking buddies, who I never cared for. I recognized him as one of the vagrants who ransacked my home that day when Elliot Jr. was supposed to be coming to get his belongings. He wore a dirty looking Dallas Cowboys jersey and outdated jeans that he had the nerve to have pressed a crease in. Chuck reeked of whiskey and exposed a mouth full of rotten teeth every time he spoke or smiled.

I couldn't help but notice someone I'd never seen before. Sitting next to Eugenia was this oddly built woman who appeared to be in her mid-late 50's. The two of them seemed to be familiar with one another, so I assumed she must have been an associate of hers. She was very nonremarkable; she had plain, oily hair that hung shoulder-length in an old school wrapped style. She wore off white striped polyester wide-legged pants with mustard-colored stripes with a mustard-colored cotton tunic-style top that showed every lump, dip and bump on her backs and bellies. I gasped when I saw her retrieve a stick of gum out of a cheap, plastic clear handbag that she actually rested on the Kelly green carpet. I thought they only issued those types of purses to prison and retail workers to prevent the entrance of contraband or stealing from stores. But it actually appeared that this woman had voluntarily worn this bag as a fashion accessory.

I snapped out of my people watching trance when I heard Elliot Jr.'s voice saying in the video, "This live ain't for those weak ass punks who don't want to fuck with the real...because it ain't no in between, you either real or you ain't! I'm a real nigga, yeah bitch, I got real receding hairline, real eyebrows, real stomach. I don't need all that fake shit to pull no bitch. Shiiit, Gucci, Fendi, Roleys, I had 'em. Fancy cars, big body Benzes, I been had that. But Imma tell you the story on how I get 'em. I got that shit the same way America was built; on the sweat and tears and on the backs of another motherfucker. Hey, it ain't no shame to my game, so you can think what you want, 'cause the motherfucker I'm speaking on agreed with that, and in my world, you gotta pay to play and you gotta pay what you weigh." Just watching and hearing him made me sick to my stomach. I was instantly disgusted by him. I wondered how he could justify being so cold, self-indulgent and entitled to my shit!

The divorce was like a blur at this point, but during the time it was going on, it was common for me to refer to him as a gold digger. But this was actually the first time I heard Elliot Jr. admit it directly out of his own mouth. I caught a glimpse of his people out of the side of my right eye, they were visibly amused. I can't say the same for the jury. Elliot Jr.'s jury of twelve consisted of two white women, six white men, two Latina women, one black man, and one black woman. The jury box was arranged in three rows of four facing the witness stand, judges' podium, stenographer's desk and the two tables for the defense on the far right and the prosecution, on the left closest to the jurors. I paid close attention to the jurors' facial expressions throughout the trial. I could see that they were not humored when Elliot bragged about having fine things and a certain lifestyle by capitalizing off of the sweat and tears of others. The lead State Prosecutor was Bradley Ratcliff. He was an attractive Caucasian man with an athletic build, blond hair, and bright green eyes. Attorney Ratcliff wore a deep blue, well-tailored Italian suit with a Texas state flag lapel pin on the left side close to his heart. He accented the All-American look with a Republican red necktie, brown wing-tipped shoes, argyle patterned socks and a Zenith El Primero Chronomaster stainless steel with a navy-blue alligator band. In the second chair sat Assistant State Prosecutor Constance Lawrence, an understated but a brilliant and cunning woman with mousy brown hair and piercing blue eyes. She was petite but carried a strong presence. She wore a cream silk shell under a plain, standard-issue business suit and black patent leather pumps, tiny diamond solitaire earrings, and a simple gold wedding band. I don't know what Craigslist ad Elliot Jr. found his lawyer on, but Vinnie Giorando Esq. looked like a character in a D-list, low-budget indie film. A 5 o'clock shadow gave him an even more unkempt appearance than his *Grease Lighting,* black stringy hair that was haphazardly pulled back in a ponytail. His shoes were among the worst I had ever seen. There's something about a man who voluntarily wears poor quality shoes. Giordano's off-black loafers were faded and badly worn over. Their cheapness was only overshadowed by the gray socks covered in white lint balls that jutted out from under his high-water pants. His suit was a polyester, all-purpose, Bar Mitzvah, funeral, courtroom dark suit that needed desperately to retire, right along with his license to practice law. The bailiff, Officer Wallace Greyson, looked like he had worked in this courtroom most of his life. Biscuits, gravy, and gravity had gotten the best of his belly, which hung down at least 6 inches over his belt. It's a wonder he could access the gun, billyclub, handcuffs or the other apparatus hooked on that belt of his. Bailiff Greyson was a bald white man with a red face, warm smile, and a long, bushy gray beard. He wore a uniform of hemmed dark green pants, a long-sleeve, celery colored shirt with an official state-issued patch on his sleeve and badge on the left side over his chest.

I hadn't expected Elliot Jr. to look like he walked off the pages of *GQ* magazine, but damn, I thought that I had at least instilled some sense of style in his ass. What a waste; his cheaply made, hard bottom shoes were poorly fashioned from synthetic leather. Throughout the trial, he wore an oversized knock-off North Face-style coat that covered a dingy white, wrinkled button-down shirt and simple off the rack slacks. He was sporting a poorly faded crew cut that left way too much on top of his head. It was a weak effort to compensate for the receding patch spreading from the crown of his head. His eyes looked drained and sunken in. I found myself asking what I had ever seen in him.

Following a compelling opening statement, Prosecutor Ratcliff had the jury on the edge of their seats to see and hear from Keilanii Jennings, the victim of a predator, gold digger and stalker. "Your Honor I would like to call Ms. Keilanii Jennings to the stand." I felt all eyes on me as my pointed red, royal blue and black Versace Medusa stilettos glided across the Kelly green carpet lined with diagonal rows of tiny golden stars. I had paired the killer shoes and matching Versace Medusa bag with a pair of navy-blue leather track pants with white and red vertical stripes that hugged my ample hips and ass. The plaid blazer with the same stripes around the ribbing on the wrists was cinched at my waist by an ornate gold button. Twenty inches of black wavy hair, courtesy of Suga Baby's new luxe hair extension business, was up into a loose bun with tendrils framing my face on either side. The style showed off my flawless skin, banging lashes, and natural glow. As far as I was concerned, this was a day to shine and Sugar Mama would not disappoint.

For some reason, once I was sworn in, poised myself on the stand and adjusted the microphone, I had the distinct feeling that the woman the jurors saw before them, was not who they expected to see. I am fabulous and flashy with no apologies, not the typical picture of a victim. It quickly became evident that I was poised and very much in control. When it came to answering questions, recalling details or clarifying any information, I was unwavering. We breezed through the initial questions that were designed to paint a picture of who I am as a professional, a mother, a wife and as a person in general. The state wanted to give the jury some insight into my character and ideally plant seeds that would compel them to empathize with me.

Bradley Ratcliff progressed my testimony to focus more on the tumultuous divorce, Elliot Jr.'s atrocities against me and my family and eventually moved to the harassment and stalking. Let me just state for the record, I am a highly educated, successful African American woman, I take pride in being the strong, H.B.I.C. and for as long as I can remember, I paid the cost to be the boss. I had voluntarily cashed out and spent lots of money on gifts, clothes, cars, and trips on my ex-husband and his funny looking ungrateful children. In the end, I had gotten played and taken advantage of. I thought that I had come to terms with everything that had happened and had truly started to move on with my life but saying these things out loud stirred something inside of me.

Throughout our entire marriage, Elliot Jr. would call me "a cold piece of work" or an "ice queen" because at times, when provoked, I come across as void of emotion. It's not that I didn't care, but I can't allow myself to engage in some small-minded mess or to succumb to being considered weak. Honey was very detached emotionally and made me work and fend for myself from the age of 14. My father had disconnected from me ever since he cheated on my mother in Germany. Kitty, Keisha, and Kairo had always envied me, made everything be about them and had their hands out. My own children had shown sides of themselves that were selfish and reckless, to say the least, so I had to put on an invisible suit of armor to navigate and dominate my own world. The last thing I would do is get caught or worse strung out on some dick. I'd witnessed sex be a powerful drug, crutch, and downfall to quite a few people, and for Elliot Jr., I believe that it became one of the strongest motivations for his obsession with me after our breakup.

Following his initial questioning, the State's Attorney requested permission to enter and publish some evidence into the record. Elliot Jr.'s attorney objected and for the next several minutes they went back and forth about the admissibility of over 30 exhibits that contained text messages from Elliot Jr.'s two phones to my two phones. It took some intense arguing, but the judge allowed Exhibits 1 to 22 correlating with my primary phone number, and Exhibits 27 to 32 that represented messages sent to my work cell. For whatever reason, Exhibits 23 to 26 were not allowed, but Bradley pressed forward.

He directed the jury's attention to their individual monitors or any one of the ten large screen TV monitors throughout the courtroom that displayed the contents of the court's overhead digital projector. He asked me to clarify which messages belonged to my phone and which were associated with Elliot Jr.'s phones. "With iPhone messages, the gray messages are incoming; those were sent from Mr. Jennings to me. The blue message is my responses, or message sent out from my phone." Initially, Elliot Jr.'s texts seemed silly and harmless; they ranged from childish to sexual, no matter what he always craved a pass to Sugarland. I was instructed to read text messages that he had sent to me over the past several months. They were listed in chronological order, enlarged for all to see. As requested, I read:

"Can I smell you one mo' gain?"

"You know Baby Boy can't suck that sweet pussy like Daddy."

"Our story gone be around for years like the Bible."

"Imma get what I was entitled to without the system."

"You still my Sugar Mama and don't even know it."

"It's exciting seeing people when they can't see you."

"What's up wit the KKK, I miss my babies with a red lip emoji."

"Nite nite Nigga."

"I'm the lead character in your life story bitch!"

"I love the KKK!"

"So, you not gone let me visit Sugarland no mo? :("

"Tell your whack ass son I got a bullet with his name on it!"

"You have no clue what's about to happen with a cloud emoji."

"You made me do this..."

"Time is running out."

"Aint shit else to lose at this point."

"See you FACE 2 FACE soon on God."

"You want attention? Imma make you famous, a legend!"

"Rest in Pieces with a target emoji."

"Keep my name out yo' mouth before your tongue get self-swallowed."

For the first few months, I really just got desensitized to it, until they started to get more and more cryptic and threatening. After speaking with the detective assigned to this case and being made aware that the state was pursuing charges against Elliot Jr., filing reports became the norm for me. Once I started gathering data, making copies, and sending emails, I began to take his threats seriously. Out of 19 pages of text messages, over a nine-month period, I only responded "Thank you", in response to his "Happy Mother's Day" text, and "please stop harassing me". When the State Prosecutor had me read the messages aloud Elliot Jr. was visibly irritated, he leaned over and whispered something to his attorney.

During cross-examination, his lawyer really made light of the meaning of the text messages and even suggested that they could have been altered, to plant a seed of doubt in the minds of the jury. Giordano tried to drill me that I had referred to Elliot Jr. as a gold digger in an email that I sent him regarding the final payout and 401K paperwork based on our divorce decree. I don't know what he was trying to prove, I admitted to having addressed him as "Dear Gold Digger" in that correspondence. I had zero remorse for characterizing him as the very thing that he is. As far as I was concerned, he was a narcissistic sociopath, a liar, and a user. I had to pay him before the divorce, during the proceedings and cash him out after the final decree was set forth. If the shoe fits, wear it.

The State's final line of testimony and questioning centered on Elliot Jr. 's drive-by at my office. Before releasing me, the lead prosecutor asked what I believed his intentions to be by showing up at my place of work. I testified that it was clear to me that he was there to scare, harass or worse, kill me. I recalled the chills running up my spine and the feeling of being frozen with panic when Elliot Jr. rode up on me holding a Glock in his hand, there's no way he came to play. I knew that from them on I needed to be on high-alert and hadn't been able to feel at peace. I shared that, for almost a year, I had felt like he was lurking, and I was always looking over my shoulder, but a part of me dismissed it as me being silly or overthinking it. That all changed that day at my office; the truth is, from Dallas and Rockwall to New Orleans, Louisiana Elliot Jr. had followed me, watched me, contacted me and as much as I downplayed my fear, he stalked me.

Elliot Jr.'s greaseball representation tried to diminish the validity of my fears by putting it out there that I hadn't blocked any of his known phone numbers. I explained that on some level, I felt that if I had blocked his texts and calls, that I would be in the dark or just a sitting duck. When he did communicate, even though it was usually cryptic and negative, at least I knew that he wasn't hiding in my garage or in a closet in my home. The man I knew and was married to for almost ten years craves an audience, he loves to get a rise or reaction out of people. I believed that if I was in imminent danger that he would get a rush out of letting me know. I had discussed this with the detective, and she said that it wasn't uncommon for victims of stalking to leave numbers unblocked. I looked right over at the jury and let them know that at first I was just annoyed by my ex's antics, especially after he had stolen my things from my house, so I had an elaborate security system installed to track and alert me of movement inside and outside of my home. As the sightings, posts, threats on me and my family's lives began to progress, I no longer took Elliot's behaviors lightly. I wanted to have a sense of whether or not he was actively watching me, but I also wanted to collect as much proof as possible for the case. At the strong suggestion of the Rockwall Police Detective, the State of Texas decided to pursue a case against Elliot Jennings Jr. for felony-level stalking. It was sobering to actually hear those words articulated, it validated my concerns and feelings.

Bradley Ratcliff made it plain to me that these charges were serious, with harsh consequences and that they would stop at nothing to get a conviction for him. They asked if I was committed to testifying, cooperating and providing access to potential witnesses. I couldn't empathize with him any longer. He used me for my fortunes and clout chasing. I gave him his divorce, turned the other cheek, paid what I was told and kept it moving. He killed my dog and showed no remorse, I bounced back. He defended his badass, socially awkward kids after they smeared dog shit all over my baby's room, I moved past that. He physically attacked my son, and we still went to Las Vegas on my dime. When my daughter was facing the legal fight of her life, Elliot Jr. exposed her mugshot online and labeled her a snitch, I had to eat that. He besmirched my mother's name by bragging about sleeping with her, my sister, cousin and closest friends, I had no choice but to let that go. He had a Black Magic spell cast on me in New Orleans and a Voodoo doll made in my likeness, and I sent it up the Mississippi River. But stalking me during my parade, rolling up on me and my staff at my office with a gun, and calling Suga Baby's cheerleading team to embarrass her by bringing up that legal shit, that was it for me. There's nothing that I wouldn't put past Elliot Jr., now I was in fear for my safety and for my life. So, would I help the State of Texas throw the book at him? Hell yeah!

Aside from me, the prosecutor called a series of witnesses to the stand, including Suga Baby, Kairo, Jozette, and Jon, my new accountant. Jon confirmed under oath that he did, in fact, see Elliot Jr. drive off in a dark vehicle from behind Kairo's white Kia in the parking lot of his place of employment. He stated that he had a clear view of the driver through the untinted windshield as he was running toward her car. Not that I had any doubt, but Jozette, proved to be extremely helpful to the prosecution. True to form, she was able to chronicle episode after episode in excruciating detail and recount every incident involving Elliot Jr. before, during and after the divorce. She testified to him jumping on Sozey, calling the office, sending notes, making threats and hanging up after breathing hard. Jozette was a credible witness and came across as cool, calm and collected. She struck a chord in me when she got a little broken up talking about the day Elliot Jr. did the drive-by. She had seen the gun too just before she grabbed my arm and pulled me in the office. Her eyes teared up as the jurors looked on while she described the feeling of her life flashing before her eyes. She confessed that during that quiet ride in the elevator up to the top floor of our office suites, she thought of her 5-year-old daughter, Sariah, and wondered what would have happened to her baby girl had she been killed that day in the midst of one of Elliot's rages. The incident had terrified her, but until that very second, she hadn't spoken of how it affected her. Jozette only worked harder to ensure that I was okay and that everything else got back to normal as soon as possible. That actually made me feel like shit, just knowing that something could have brought danger and tragedy to an innocent person and family that I am responsible for. Once the state had excused Jozette, Giordano stood to cross-examine her but paused, flipped through a couple of pages and declined to approach the stand only saying, "No questions of the witness, your honor."

Elliot Jr. 's Dial-a-Lawyer only asked Jon one or two insignificant questions and he passed on cross-examining Jozette. I guess he must have counted on Kairo being easy prey for him. "Your Honor, I'd like to call Miss Kairo Scott to the stand." I could tell by his demeanor and questions off the bat that he planned on giving Kairo the blues. The irony is, although my sister is good at melting down and making every situation about her, much to my surprise, she held it together pretty well. It was like Kairo had practiced remaining calm and staying on the topic just so she could say what she had been holding on to for over a year. She got the golden opportunity when the defense attorney asked her about the nature of her relationship with Elliot Jennings Jr. Giordano tried to break her by posing back to back questions like "Is it true that you are envious of Kelanii because you had intimate feelings for her ex-husband?" and "Were you truly afraid when you saw Mr. Jennings in the parking lot that day or was you merely upset because he rejected you after two slept together?" Ratcliff yelled, "Objection, your Honor! Counsel is badgering the witness!" Even the judge had a shocked look on his face when he responded, "Sustained." The stenographer was typing extra fast, the bailiff seemed to adjust his bellies and the jury was all tuned in. That was all she wrote, Kairo came undone.

She screamed to the top of her lungs, nostrils flared and eyes bulging out of their sockets; she looked right in Elliot's direction and yelled, "You are a liar and the truth ain't in you! You are the scum of the earth...I watched you play games with my sister, mistreat her kids, ransack her house…" Giordano directed his response to the judge, "Your Honor, can you instruct the witness to…" before he could even finish his objection Kairo kicked back in, "You said all that stuff about my niece, defamed my mother's name and you lied on me!" She was seething, tears were pouring down her face and her hair suddenly seemed disheveled. Sweat was pouring from her forehead and armpits. The judge asserted himself, saying, "Miss Scott, that is enough!" Kairo said sobbing, "But your Honor, this man is evil and he's dangerous!" Judge Atkinson said, "Miss Scott, you need to calm down and control yourself." Kairo was shaking as she tried to compose herself.

The defense continued, "Miss Scott, I know this is difficult to you, but I have to ask, has Mr. Jennings ever physically harmed you?" Kairo looked at the judge, at the jury and then back at Elliot Jr. "That man has hurt everyone in my family, he put it in my baby sister's mind that he slept with her closest friends and he lied about sleeping with me!" She then locked eyes with Elliot Jr. and proclaimed, "I never slept with you and you know it! Leave my family alone!" Frustrated, the defense attorney said, "Your Honor, can you instruct the witness to answer the question?" He looked in Kairo's direction and yelled: "Miss Scott, you will only answer the question, nothing more, I will not warn you again!" My poor sister looked overcome with exhaustion, but she accomplished what she came to do. In her mind, she had sworn on a stack of Bibles, faced the enemy in a court of law, and spoke her truth. At that moment Kairo was more than just an overly dramatic person, seeking attention, she was my big sister. I was proud of her for defending herself, and in her own way standing up for me. It was the first time in our lives that I'd ever felt like my sister had really shown up for me, and with no selfish motives.

Early on during trial preparation, the State Prosecutor went back and forth on whether or not to put Suga Baby on the stand. There was genuine concern about the jury being prejudiced if the defense brought up the investigation and arrest of my daughter concerning her role in the crime spree that ended with an innocent man losing his life. She had been on house arrest since her uncle had arranged for her release, pending a Grand Jury hearing. Her uncle Randoph II had represented her throughout the entire ordeal and I was eternally grateful to him. On one hand, Suga Baby is an 18-year-old, former cheerleading champion, entering her first year of fashion design school. She is a petite, beautiful, soft-spoken and well-mannered young lady who the State Prosecutors believed would pull on the heartstrings of the jury. On the other hand, my little princess had been arrested in connection with a heinous crime and implicated as the owner of the getaway car and possible driver. It was a clear concern that the defense would most likely use this information to discredit her character and slant the jury's perception of me.

A few weeks before the trial began, Suga Baby and I were about to sit down to dinner when my brother called and announced that he wanted to come right over to deliver some important news about the case. Both my daughter and I were nervous, so we didn't say much during our meal. As soon as Randolph

II arrived, Suga suddenly became nauseous, she jumped up from the table and proceeded to vomit in my master bathroom. I gave him a hug and went in to check on her. She was splashing water on her face and said that she was okay, just overcome with nerves. Until all this shit happened, my baby girl's life had been a charmed one, but this past year had been very stressful. With all the stuff on social media, the reality that her so-called friends had taken a man's life while she was at a Big Sean concert and were now in TDC serving life sentences, her long-time star-athlete boyfriend had left for his three semester at the University of Alabama on a full-ride football scholarship, having to wear an ankle monitor and sit out on her senior year activities and watching her mother go through so much with the only father-figure she ever knew, Suga Baby was under a great deal of pressure.

When she and I sat back down at the dining room table, my brother pulled out a few papers from his briefcase and gave us the biggest smile. "Princess, I'm pleased to tell you that you are a free young lady." We both looked at him dumbfounded but could see the excitement and joy on his face. He explained that all charges against Suga Baby had been dropped. There hadn't been enough evidence for the City of Dallas District Attorney to pursue a conviction. Thanks to our social media posts from the concert, related credit card records and corroborating statements from the two guys who admitted that they acted alone,

Suga Baby was in the clear. I read the documents as Randolph II explained that the young men were adamant that neither Lexus nor Suga Baby had any knowledge of what they were involved in and that they had asked to use her car to go to the recording studio on the night in question. It was the best news I heard in a long time. More than anything I was elated that my baby was given back the opportunity to live her life to the fullest and to pursue her dreams.

The next day when we went up to the Dallas Police Department, Suga Baby got nauseous again while a female officer was removing the ankle monitor. When I signed the equipment release form and went into the bathroom to check on her, I saw her reflection clearly in the mirror. She was holding her belly and I noticed the bump. We had planned to go to her favorite restaurant, Grand Luxe, for dinner. It had been a while since she could even be out past 7 pm. We were going to celebrate her freedom and discuss her plans for the future. It seemed that now we'd have to discuss the new life growing in her womb and how she planned on taking care of it.

With the past behind her, the State's Attorney felt confident that Suga Baby would make a strong witness. He couldn't have been more right. Not only was she poised and succinct in her responses, but she also came off as genuine and innocent. It's easy for her to be seen as delicate based on her appearance. At just under 5 feet tall, well put together and polite, she was the kind of witness that members of a jury would most definitely empathize with. She testified about the Mexican candy delivery, being humiliated online by her former stepfather and that he killed her dog. That was the clincher; you know white people don't play when it comes to dogs and cats. One of the blond hair female jurors actually cried when Suga Baby described coming home from the Olympics and Diamond being gone with no real explanation, no burial or way to say goodbye.

When she was asked about Elliot Jr.'s call to CheerStar Athletics, it was as if everything had built up and exploded. Suga Baby's voice quivered as she described how embarrassed she was to know that the man she once looked up to and even loved as a dad would stoop so low as to call and smear her name to her teammates and coaches she looked up to. She admitted to the jury that she is not perfect, she makes mistakes and has a lot to learn about life. She confessed that she had some really dark moments and how her self-esteem had been impacted by the humiliation of her friends and their parents giving her the side-eye or asking her straight up if she is a snitch or worse, a murderer. If all twelve men and women hadn't been convinced that Elliot Jr. was an asshole before my baby took the stand, her testimony put the nail in his coffin.

The state rested its case in the late afternoon of the second day. Judge Henley Atkinson adjourned court and told us that the proceedings would resume at 9 am the next day. He thanked the jury, reminded them not to discuss the case with anyone and dismissed everyone for the day.

By the time Shiloh, Skylar, Kairo and I sat down and ordered cocktails and appetizers at Ruth Chris Steakhouse, we were all waiting to exhale! The handsome server delivered the first round of lemon drop martinis with Ciroc Ten Vodka in chilled glasses with sugared rims and assured us that he would be right back with our chilled shrimp cocktail and sizzling blue crab cakes appetizers. The ladies were buzzing and going on and on about the trial and all of Elliot's bullshit. I purposely tabled the discussion about the courtroom fashion crimes until Bella arrived. She was the self-proclaimed "fashion police " and would get quite a kick out of hearing all the petty details.

We'd just hung up, she said she was only a few minutes out. Belle was the Creative Director and wardrobe stylist for popular Dallas WFFA news anchor Demetria Obilor, so she couldn't make it to court on the first day. She had texted, called and insisted that I send her photos of my courtroom looks. I understood her work schedule and I knew that she was most definitely there in spirit. I hadn't heard from Kitty or Keisha, but I was a little surprised that neither of them showed up at all. True to form, Kairo was at the center of the conversation. I let her have it; after all, she had really shown her support and had my back in the courtroom and that meant a lot to me. We all toasted to her going off on Elliot Jr.

then Shiloh and Skylar recapped the entire testimony and all the highlights like they were seasoned, court reporters. Just listening to the chatter and recalling everything that had come out during testimony felt like an out of body experience.

By the time Bella arrived, I downed my second martini, made eyes with that fine-ass waiter and we ordered our entrees. I was starting to feel more like myself. Bella had helped me pick out my outfit, but this was the first time she saw it all together and how I had accessorized it, so she was loving it. Bella got hyped about all things fashion, so she damn near fell out of her chair when Shiloh started clowning Elliot's family and attorney about what they were wearing. When she got around to Eugenia's friend's fashions, Skyla quickly corrected her, letting us know the old lady was Elliot Jr.'s new squeeze. She told us that she noticed the woman reached in her clear plastic handbag and pulled out a lip balm, Elliot Jr. motioned for her to let him use it. As far as Skylar was concerned, that was far too intimate a move for a platonic supporter or family member. Kairo couldn't agree more and said that when we were all dismissed for the day and everyone was getting up, she reached her hand over the partition bar between the pews and the defense table, and he grabbed it. As I listened, it all clicked for me too. That chick was Elliot Jr.'s newest victim; boy, what a downgrade. I just shook my head, devoured my filet Oscar, cooked to perfection, topped with succulent crabmeat and asparagus and ordered a third martini.

By 8:45 am, the courtroom was filling up. At 8:55 am, the jurors were escorted in and getting settled. Bradley Ratcliff pulled me to the side and explained that it was now time for Mr. Jennings to present his defense. He assured me that it wasn't looking too good for Elliot and that the defense didn't appear to be calling anyone to testify on his behalf. He reminded me that regardless of the outcome, that he was proud of me for standing up for myself and commended me on doing a great job the day before. Elliot Jennings Jr. took the stand as the sole witness for the defense. He stood tall confidently raising his right hand, placing his left hand on the Bible help by Bailiff Greyson and repeated loudly as if he were on a television game show "...the truth and nothing but the truth, so help me God!" There was buzzing energy in the courtroom, it was as if everyone was eager to hear from the character that they had heard so much about.

Attorney Giordano wasted no time in getting Elliot to describe the nature of our relationship and how we met. We all listened intently as he boasted about meeting me through a mutual friend named Jackie, who allegedly shared with him that I was a meal ticket. He testified that Jackie confided in him that I was about my money and that I was lonely because my baby's daddy had just died. He added that Jackie told him I was known to break bread on younger men. At first, I just chuckled to myself, because it's true that

I have a weakness for fine young men, Elliot Jr. was exaggerating, because our hooking up was nothing like that. He went on to say that after talking on the phone a couple of times, I invited him to my house for dinner. Elliot Jr. testified that after I put Suga Baby to bed in her crib, he and I had hot and heavy sex, and as "compensation" I gave him $3,000. I felt sick to my stomach. According to this bottom feeder, I was a woman who didn't get very much attention and wasn't as attractive as I am today. He said that at the time I was over 300 pounds, about a decade older than him, the edges of my hair were thinning and that I needed dental work. He boasted that he was about 150 pounds, good looking, physically fit and a known stallion. He had the nerve to call himself a gigolo and stated on the record in a court of law and boasted that his job was getting paid for sex and companionship. He said that I was aware of this and agreed to pay with no qualms. I watched the faces of his mother, The Chief and his presumed lady as he bragged about bartering companionship and sexual favors for cold hard cash. They were not amused. The Chief dropped his head in shame. His mother put her right hand over her frontal lobe massaging her temples with her finger and thumb. The girlfriend could have been sold for a penny. She wore a two-piece denim look from the '70s made of patches of different shades of denim and some cheap-looking wedge heels covered in dark blue denim. She looked both pissed at Elliot Jr.'s stupid ass and embarrassed at the same damn time. I had to catch myself from snickering when she peered over at me with such venom.

Giordano just allowed his client to go on about how Elliot Jr. and I had an "understanding" with regard to our relationship in terms of this so-called arrangement. According to this fool, he applied for a job, I accepted his application and put him on the payroll. I knew this wasn't true, so that part didn't hurt me, but it was humiliating for me to have to listen to a man that I once promised to love until death does us part, reduce our union to something so trite and transactional. I was just glad the jury got to hear this shit with their own ears. The crazy thing is Elliot Jr. couldn't keep up with his own story.

He contradicted himself so many times; he went from claiming that I paid him for sex and to keep up appearances, to insisting that he gave me everything he could and that he worked to help build my businesses and was entitled to so much more than the $8K monthly salary I had put him on. Which was it, were you a paid gigolo or were you an underpaid laborer in my Home Health Care business? Anyhoo, the fact remained that this case; *THE STATE OF TEXAS Vs. ELLIOT ``GOLD DIGGER" JENNINGS JR.* had nothing to do with our marriage or the terms of our divorce settlement. Once he was done making a spectacle and a complete ass of himself on the stand, his poor excuse for counsel turned him over to the state. Bradley Ratcliff tore his ass up!

He asked Elliot Jr. about the threats made on me

and my family and him being caught on security camera pulling off from my home. The prosecutor had him read aloud the posts he made to social media and his repeated mentions of the KKK. With the exception of the KKK, Elliot's responses to all questions were something lame, like, "It wasn't even like that, man, she know how we do!", "We always got down like that, she trippin!" or his favorite, "She know I didn't mean none of that". The last time he used that excuse, he looked directly at me and repeated it, "Tell 'em Keilanii, you know I ain't mean none of that shit…" Ratcliff had rattled his feathers and his overinflated ego and tough-guy exterior was starting to deteriorate. The prosecution yelled, "Your Honor, instruct the witness to address the court only!" Judge Atkinson gave Elliot a firm warning, then motioned for Ratcliff to continue.

"Mr. Jennings, can I draw your attention to State's Exhibit 22; may I publish for the court, your Honor?" Atkinson nodded and said yes. Once it was established the Elliot Jr. recognized and then read aloud the text message "I Love the KKK", Ratcliff asked, "Mr. Jennings, can you explain this text message 'I Love the KKK'?" The defendant pulled the mic in closer to his mouth, cleared his throat and said in a more pronounced tone, "Can you hear me? Can y'all hear me now? What sense do it make, me as a black man in the United States of America, hell, in Texas for that matter, saying that I love the actual KKK? I was referring to Keilanii's sister Kairo, her cousin Kitty and her so-called bestie Keisha. See she always bad mouthed me to them and tried to put a nigga down and play me in front of them. She thought they all had her back but they was playing on my team. Even her own sister would complain to me about the way she treated her. My ex-wife be talking down to people and shit, so they vent to me or come to cry on my shoulder. That's basically how it happened. Keisha and I had an ongoing relationship for years, she gave me all kinds of intel. And me and her cousin Kitty, that was just a lay, but we slipped up one time and she got pregnant. Keilanni paid for the abortion and didn't even know it. I guess she told them too much about my skills in the bed because they all wanted a taste!" He was actually animated and proud with his chest poked out. The Chief stood up and removed himself from the courtroom.

Just as Ratcliff was about to pose the next question Elliot Jr. added, "She always thought she was better than everybody else, they would tell me all kinds of shit, you see her road dogs Kitty and Keisha ain't here in court, that's probably why!" Judge Atkinson gave him an ice-cold look and Elliot put up his hands and motioned as if he was zipping his lips closed. Ratcliff kept going through the text messages, the witness testimony and all the evidence stacked up against him.

Just before 1:30 pm, the state eventually addressed the fateful incident outside of my office. By this time Elliot Jr. had lost his zeal, the reality of the situation seemed to be kicking in. He wasn't looking like the same boastful gigolo who had gotten such a kick out of himself. "Mr. Jennings, tell me about the day that you drove to the known office building of your ex-wife, one Ms. Keilanii Jennings". The courtroom was so quiet you could hear a pin drop. Everyone was tuned in, but this time all the seats had filled up. It was after lunch and most dockets had been cleared so there were lots of other attorneys, law enforcement and people there to support me. I had to do a double-take but then noticed that in the back row on the defense's side, closest to the door sat Sozey. Like his mamma, he was dressed to the nines, in one of the outfits, he was supposed to rock at my Fabulous 50th, no doubt. But at that moment, all that didn't matter, what was important to me was that he was there. He just nodded and shot me a cool little smile. I know that boy loves me, there may be hope for him yet.

When Elliot Jr. spoke, his voice cracked this time. Ratcliff asked him to speak directly into the microphone. He said, "I'm not gone try to sugar coat it yall, I was wrong. I had no business going up to that place that day. I, I just don't know, it's like this whole situation done just went too far. It wasn't supposed to be like this. Yeah, I was mad, and I was frustrated with how things were going in our relationship and everything. But I was never going to go through with no divorce. I was just trying to scare her into tightening shit up, I'm sorry, my bad. I mean just wanted my wife to get her son in check in to stop treating me like the help. I was her husband and I wanted an equal say. So much stuff just got out of hand. I made some bad moves; she made some bad moves. I feel messed up for saying those things about her daughter 'cause that was my baby too. I known that girl since she was a tiny little baby and it was like they all gave me their butt to kiss and I was pissed. Then my ex started fooling around with my nephew and I just couldn't take the thought of that. It seem like my text messages kept getting ignored or misunderstood, I couldn't get no solid advice or help from the KKK, I sent flowers and that got tooken the wrong way, so I was stuck. Honest to God, I went to New Orleans as a last-ditch effort to try and talk to Keilanii and maybe just see if we could come to some common ground, but I saw Baby Boy go in her hotel and I was pissed. I watched her lead that parade with all the feathers and the band and the people partying and stuff and I was sick. That used to be us on trips and stuff. I was supposed to be there with her...to celebrate, to kick it and have fun and make her laugh like I used to. But it didn't work out that way. I swear when I got back to Dallas and went up to her job, my only intention was to talk to her, to try to get her to see me in another light. I got a job now, I'm making decent money, plus I still got the upholstery shop. I got a new whip and I was just planning on rolling up and speaking to her before she sent into her office. Everything just went haywire when Kairo saw me first. Man, that woman is nuts, she started panicking and screaming and doing the most. I pulled up behind her and rolled down the window so she could see that it was me and I could try to calm her down and ask if her sister was there yet. Before I had the chance to say anything, this dude started running toward my vehicle and out of instinct I pulled out my piece. I sped off to avoid any confrontation and circled the building trying to get my head back right when I saw her. Keilanii was moving so fast across the walkway I sped up with a try to catch her, to get her attention and say hey or something, but I could tell by the look in her eyes that it was too late, I had fucked up."

Shortly after his testimony, the state declined any further questions and the defense rested. Both sides presented their closing statements, Giordano gave a lackluster final plea on Elliot Jr. 's behalf and Assistant State Prosecutor Constance Lawrence shut it down with her rousing recap, statistics on domestic violence and increase in stalker-related murders and urged the jury to return a guilty verdict. The judge carefully explained to the jury the rules of law concerning stalking, the burden of proof, what must and must not be considered and sent them out to deliberate. Once the bailiff cleared the jurors and Judge Atkinson left the bench, the people on the other side of the bar where we sat were buzzing. Law clerks, reporters, attorneys, family members, and other witnesses were all speaking in hushed tones. As Sozey was about to make his way to me, I motioned to meet me outside, I followed the flow of the small sea of people going out of the right door, while others from my side exited on the left side. I joined Attorney Lawrence, who gave me a smile and a wink, but as luck would have it, I ended up directly in front of Elliot Jr.'s newest victim. His mother was behind her and Eugenia was a couple of people to the rear of her. I could feel the heat and negative vibes permeate from her body. She had to be at least 4 inches taller than me naturally, 6 with those ugly ass denim-covered mules. I could swear her breath was straightening out the waves in my expensive extensions. She reeked of cheap cologne, probably purchased from CVS. I heard Elliot and Eugenia's mother murmur under her breath, "That bitch!" but I kept it moving with a pleasant look plastered on my face. They had never seen Sugar sweat or rattled and they were not about to today.

When I finally made it out of the two sets of double doors, my tribe was a sight for sore eyes. Suga Baby gave me the biggest hug, she said, "I'm so proud of you, Mamma, I know I can be a brat, but I truly do appreciate everything you have done for me. Thank you for teaching me to be accountable for my own actions, to choose my friends more wisely and for protecting us." I knew that my little girl was going to have to grow up a bit faster than I had hoped, but I had no doubt that she would be just fine. I wasn't going to raise her child for her, but I would for damn sure teach her how. Shiloh and Skylar were there with these priceless looks on their faces, their eyes motioning toward Elliot Jr.'s new lady. I laughed, gave them a hug and we talked briefly about how much we are looking forward to getting back to work and the big rollout we were planning for the next quarter.

Bella was able to make it after the morning DFFA morning news segment. She admired my day-two ensemble, a black cashmere crisscrossed, long-sleeved sweater, form-fitting zebra print Yves Saint Laurent skirt, and Corvette red Alexander McQueen shoe booties accented with my black Hilde Palladino shoulder bag. My ride or die Jozette stood close by, she squeezed my hand and quietly asked if I needed anything, I told her that I was fine. Kairo was about to get all riled up and emotional when I hugged her. She started to defend herself again, but I stopped her and assured her that we were fine. Last but not least, was my Lil' Sozey; he was leaned up against the wall rocking an Escada T-shirt and jeans with one foot against the wall and the other on the ground showing off his fresh Tom Ford Jago sneakers. He gave me this cool head nod motion and said: "You got it, Sugar, what's up witcha?" I said, "You see it, you know how we do." He gave a little grin and said, "Ol' boy ain't never deserve my mama no way. But for real, though, I know you always had a lil' nig'...I know you always had my back and I ain't really been livin' up to that. My bad, but on God I promise you Imma make you proud one of these days. I'm thinking about going for my masters...now that would be real gangsta!" I was glad to hear that his head was still screwed on straight, and although he still had a ways to go, I know that my son has the DNA and good sense to be great at anything he puts his mind to.

So much of Elliot Jr.'s testimony was total bullshit, but the point he made about Kitty and Keisha not being there actually rang true. After all that we've been through, all that we've shared and all that I've done for those heifers, they didn't bother to come. There's no way that I would have not shown up to support them for such an important experience. In fact, neither of them had even called in the past few days to check on me or see how things were going, shit; maybe they didn't need an update because they had gotten first-hand information from Elliot Jr. himself.

We had made our way to the cafeteria and grabbed some coffee on the first level of the courthouse, when I noticed through the window, The Chief coming back in the courthouse preparing to go through the metal detector. There was a woman ahead of him loading her purse and belongings on the conveyor belt, and he seemed to be agitated and in a hurry.

The ding of the elevator snapped me out of staring, Bradley Ratcliff's law clerk Cindy exited the elevator and spotted me right away. "Great! I was coming to for you, the verdict is in! Usually when the jury comes back with a verdict so quickly that means he's guilty. No promises, just saying." I motioned for everyone to come on. We quickly filed into the elevator, the last to enter was The Chief, he paused before stepping in but I guess he had gotten word that the verdict was in, so we all just rode up to the third floor in awkward silence.

Suga Baby grabbed my hand. Judge Atkinson adjusted his glasses then ordered Elliot Jr. and Attorney Giordano to stand. Then said, "Members of the jury, have you reached a verdict?" The jury spokesperson, an older Latina woman, said, "yes your Hono,r we have." He responded, "Members of the jury, in the case of The State of Texas vs. Elliot Jennings Jr., on the count of third-degree felony stalking, what say you?" The spokesperson read, "Your Honor, the members of this jury find the defendant guilty." The judge said, "Members of the jury, this court dismisses you and thank you for a job well done".

Ratcliff turned backward, facing me and made a power fist gesture. The defense counsel was leaned in whispering something to Elliot Jr. whose head was down on the table with his hands on his head. Eugenia was grumbling, "This some bullshit," while consoling their mother who had burst into tears. Elliot Jr.'s lady was shaking her head with her arms folded in front of her rocking back and forth. The Chief had disappeared.

"Order in the court!" Judge Atkinson yelled. "I will have order in my court, or you will be removed." Bailiff Greyson moved closer to the left side of the courtroom where the commotion had started to percolate and motioned for Elliot to stand back up. Everyone settled down then the Judge proceeded.

"Mr. Jennings, you have been found guilty by a jury of your peers and convicted of third-degree felony stalking. This is a serious offense that the State of Texas does not take lightly, sir. You will be taken into custody immediately." Elliot Jr. lost temporary control of his body and slumped over, nearly falling to his knees. As Greyson and two other court officers grabbed and pulled him back to stand him on his feet, he looked over at me, for the first time since the trial started, and I made eye contact with him. With tears in his eyes, he said: "For real, Sugar?" Judge Atkinson added, "Mr. Jennings, you will return to this court in 90 days for sentencing". Elliot Jr. was still in disbelief as they placed the handcuffs on his wrists and escorted him into the holding cell to await transport to the maximum-security Texas Detention Center.

So many mixed emotions swirled through my body at that instant. I vacillated between being in shock, feeling victorious to being in disbelief that shit had gotten to this level. While I was glad that Elliot Jr. would have to answer for all that he had done to me and my loved ones, oddly enough, I believe much of this testimony toward the end when he confessed that shit had gone way too far and that he never really wanted to break up in the first place. I know that I can be an "ice queen" and very bossy at times, but I wasn't a bad wife and we did have lots of good times together, even long before the marriage. We had a real relationship, not a paid arrangement. I didn't tie the knot, to end up tying it into a noose around his neck, but Elliot Jr. had hung himself. If I'm being honest, I would have most likely ignored the texts, made light of the Mexican candy and other stuff, but when he went after Suga Baby and came up to my office with a gun, I had no choice but to go at him with every fiber of my being. I have never been one to cry wolf or involve the police or the courts in my personal affairs; that goes against the very street code that I was brought up in, but this wasn't on me; Mr. Gold Digger had dug his own ditch and now he had to suffer the consequences.

If I'm being honest, I used to wish death on him. Every time I drove past a wreck, I would pray it was him. Despite how I feel about his kids, I would never do anything to hurt, exploit or admonish them publicly in any way. He didn't extend the same courtesy to me, that's why I can sleep at night knowing the only gigolo-ing Elliot Jr. gone be doing is selling his ass for some Ramen noodles and Hot Cheetos. I have no regrets, and as far as I'm concerned, he got what was coming to him. I've always maintained that my venom or hatred for him wasn't about the money. My livelihood, survival and lavish lifestyle were never contingent upon him. And he was right, I am 10 years older than him, I was significantly heavier when we met, but thanks to changing my eating habits, Dr. Miracles in Beverly Hills, Dallas' top cosmetic dentist and my dream team glam squad keeping me all the way together, the Sugar he was sprung on even then, was 100 times sweeter now and that made him sick to his heart. Just know, even with a few extra pounds and inches, I was fly, flossy and bossy before I ever laid eyes on Elliot Jennings Jr. and would be long after they lock him up and throw away the key. I still had to work to maintain what I had and grind for what I wanted. That was the tangible stuff. As for the immeasurable things, I suffered humiliation, lost some time, dignity, pride and a few relationships that I thought I'd always have. Even with all of that, I could have possibly accepted his remorse, but the attacks against my children were violations written in blood that could never be forgiven or forgotten. As far as I'm concerned, I was lucky to have exited that situation with what I did. I can cut my losses and move on. A lot of times when women find themselves in a gold-digging, opportunistic situation, it's because she does have self-esteem issues, believes that her choices are limited or feel that she won't find a man to genuinely love her for who she is rather than what she has to offer. There's a huge misconception that sugar mamas are wealthy, unattractive or lonely cougars who have the expendable income to lace a nigga with money and all kinds of nice things.

The reality is gold diggers prey on women of all socio-economic backgrounds. Trust me, there's a beautiful sister in her mid-30s, well educated, working a regular 9 to 5, paying her car note, student loans and maintaining the mortgage on her first home. From the outside, it looks like she got her shit together.

When you take a closer look under the hood, you see that while she's at work, she got a black ass good for nothing nigga laying in the bed she bought, eating her snacks and watching Sports Center on her 55-inch. The only thing he's bringing to the relationship is some dick. She's convinced herself like I did, that he has potential and she likes the idea of having that warm body to hold her and hard cock to ride at night.

Let's not forget about our homegirl in her late 20s; she has three kids, lives in rent-controlled, Section 8 housing, collects electronic food stamps and braids hair in her living room as a side hustle. As a single parent she struggles to make ends meet, she's been in one abusive relationship after another, and deep down believes that ain't no nigga gon' really want her with all those kids. So, she allows her baby daddy to come back and forth, treat her any kind of way and smoke his weed in her place, despite her complaints. She doesn't hear shit from him through the holidays but come January, all of a sudden, it's "Cuffing Season" again, he wants to Netflix and chill and posts them boo'd up on the Gram. Suddenly the flaky baby daddy turns in #BaeGoals, but the truth is, it ain't #CuffingSeason it's #TaxSeason. Ol' boy is getting in position to tap into that fat U.S. Income Tax check! He does her wrong all year long but does all the right shit just before it's time for the Earned Income Credit to kick in. These kinds of niggas are just varying degrees of GOLD DIGGERS and I Keilanii Jennings is calling these bastards out once and for all.

I know that if I wanted things to be better, I had to do better and I wanted my daughter to know that no matter what, she didn't have to accept less than what she deserves from a man. I'm determined to help her avoid many of the pitfalls out here and to spot a gold digger coming a mile away. She had me shook for a minute there, but I can truly say that she's made a big comeback in my book and has done a lot to regain my trust and support. She's doing extremely well in fashion design school and with Grand Baby Luxe on the way, Suga Baby's more determined than ever to pursue her career in the fashion and beauty industries. She launched what's proving to be a very lucrative hair extension company. That close call with her freedom taught my daughter some tough lessons on trusting so-called friends and earning the privilege to live that affluenza lifestyle versus taking it off the sweat and tears of others. With my help and the support of her loving boyfriend, one of the NFL draft's top prospects, my princess is preparing a kingdom for our royal addition to thrive in.

Once the dust settled with the trail, Sozey followed through on his decision to pursue a master's degree. He really surprised me when he applied for Federal Financial Aid, got a FASFA Unsubsidized Loan with Jozette's help, and enrolled in the Business Administration program at Texas A&M University all by himself. He even used the funds leftover after taking care of the tuition to partner with a couple of classmates out there to open a recording studio.

He finally unblocked me on Instagram, so I've seen pictures, and some video of the studio. Sozey is still smoking weed like a chimney but it feels like he's focused and serious about staying on track this time. He even promised to pay me back for the $4K clothes he charged on my accounts. I can't say that I believe that will ever happen, nor do I require that, but at least he acknowledged the situation. He sent me a $CashApp request the other day for $100, I thought about it for a couple of hours then I went ahead and sent it. He is my son and he is trying, that's all I ask. He instantly replied with a bright red heart.

As for Baby Boy, he will always be in my life on some level. As she was making her transition, I promised Tangi that I would be there for her girls and make sure that no matter what, they would be taken care of. Other than missing their momma dearly, they haven't missed a beat. No one had any clue that a relationship would spark between Ross and me, and God knows that was never my intention, so I don't have any guilt behind things getting physical between us. But to keep it all the way real, Baby Boy could never be the caliber of man to stand beside me for real. Even with his recent promotion to Plant Manager and maintaining his landscaping business, the only thing I could ever see him as in the "maintenance man". Plus, I have a nagging suspicion that deep down he felt some kind of way that his uncle had to do a five-year bid behind fucking with me. Even still, that didn't stop Baby Boy from coming for my nectar. He was going to be in for a rude awakening though because I've begun accepting applications and conducting interviews for a qualified Sugar Daddy and I was getting very close to choosing a candidate, or two for full-time positions.

I went ahead and canceled that Sam's Club membership. I don't think Elliot Jr. will need it up in the TDC for the next five years. He had allowed his 24-Hour Fitness lapse anyway due to non-payment, but now he had all the time in the world to concentrate on his figure. If I know Mr. Jennings, the way I think I do, he's going to do anything and everything in his power and use his gift of gab to keep old girl on the hook, his corner and putting money on his books. At least we know that she already owns a clear plastic purse to carry in her approved belongings and an outfit to match his prison blues during visitation. They would look really nice in prison photos.

Thanks to my ex, my threshold for games and BS has been far surpassed. I changed my patterns in dealing with men. I'd always been naturally generous; if I eat, we all eat, if I ride good, we all ride good mentality. I felt that since I had it, I was obligated to share it with the people closest to me. As a result of all that Elliot Jr. put me through, that perception has changed permanently. My guard remains in the 'up' position, I spot users more easily and let me tell you, my tolerance is zero. I've come to accept that being a Sugar Mama hasn't gotten me anywhere but screwed over. You try to be nice and do kind things, but for gold diggers, it's never enough. I believed that I was helping them do better. I learned the hard way that you can't make somebody be or do something they aren't.

Since the age of 14, I'd figured out how to get the bag, but I hadn't factored in being the victim of a vulture. Even still, I couldn't dwell in the bitter, life for me had only gotten sweeter because of it. So, for me, it wasn't a loss, it was a powerful lesson. Honey always said, "God bless the child who's got his own", but take it from Sugar, don't fool with that child who ain't got shit.

"The very dogs were all asleep, and the flies, drunk with moist sugar in the grocer's shop, forgot their wings and briskness, and baked to death in dusty corners of the window."

—Charles Dickens

The End

Author's Note

THE LONGER YOU live, the better you will come to understand that your life is not truly yours. Yes, we all have desires and an inner drive to find fulfillment. The truest reward, however, is discovering our purpose to serve others through the lives we lead. Whether you realize it or not, we are all in a position to serve through our actions and words. The will to activate and walk in this purpose is completely on you. While some give of themselves on a grand scale, others may do so by sowing seeds of wisdom, knowledge and time. Giving doesn't have to be tangible in the physical sense to be impactful and impressionable in the spiritual sense. Some might say that I learned this lesson the hard way, but I say experience is the best teacher and I'm a star pupil!

It is my prayer that you find this novel intriguing and inspiring. It was my pleasure to co-write Sugar Mama: A Keilanii Jennings Saga with the intention of freeing anyone trapped in an exploitative situation by someone who they believe was supposed to love and care for them.

I encourage you to always strive to walk in the light and pray that your journey is peaceful. While mine was at times a tumultuous one that certainly had its peaks and troughs, I've learned to never be shocked or surprised by the acts of humans or the void of their souls. I've seen behaviors at their finest and their worst, so rarely does anyone or anything take me off-guard.

I can bear witness to overcoming the ploys of Lucifer and plots of his treachery. I accept that not everyone will subscribe to my philosophy of our path and purpose here on this earth, I can only offer my perspective and speak my truth with the most genuine and pure intentions.

My experience has compelled me to ponder on the origins of the gold digger or user mentality. Jilted men are known to gripe about women who exploit them for money, material gain and defamation of character. It's rarely discussed when men do the same thing to the fairer sex. One of my paramount goals in approaching this story was to start a dialogue regarding this gender disparity and to advise that the exploitation doesn't have to be over the top. Gold diggers exist at all income brackets and socio-economic levels. Victimization can be as simple as a man living with a woman in her government-sponsored housing. It can look like him eating off of your taxpayer grocery coupons or EBT food card while contributing minimally to nothing in the relationship or household. I'm here to tell you that sex is not sufficient reciprocation, and while just getting by may enough for him, let that never be a sufficient end game for you. I'm here to tell you that you deserve so much more!

This book is for anyone who has looked for love in the wrong places, got catfished or used before knowing better. This is for the victims of gold-diggers who are too wounded and humiliated to admit it or discuss it. Sugar Mama is for those who love and trust their family and friends with loyalty to a fault, only to find that their real interest is self-preservation versus truth. This is for the ones who have loved unconditionally and never felt the reciprocation.

I salute you and want you to know that you can continue to love unconditionally and walk in the light to restore your soul. I want you to know that no one's life meaning is greater than yours and that loving yourself is imperative to everything worth achieving. And even though you have endured pain and disappointment at the hands of the one(s) you loved, I urge you to forgive and move on. Life is too short to harbor resentment. Moreover, I assure you, they are not worth your energy. Take it from me, Karma handles everything. I've seen life come full circle enough times to know with certainty that this is true. This constant is evidenced so colorfully and cleverly in Keilanii's next saga; full of new adventures and fabulosity! You just wait and see...

> **"Your fair discourse hath been as sugar, making the hard way sweet and delectable."**
>
> —William Shakespeare

LALANII WILSON JONES

The Dallas, Texas-based entrepreneur is a celebrated professional who has found immense success in the Home Health Care, Hospice, and Child Care industries. In addition to owning and operating thriving facilities, brands, and businesses throughout Texas, Lalanii also runs Mogul 24/7, a prominent lifestyle, luxury event planning and entertainment business. In addition to adding bricks to her growing empire, she cultivates other moguls on the rise and enjoys traveling the world, decadent food, fashion, and cheering on her beloved Cowboys! Most of all, she appreciates spending quality time with her family, especially her new Grand Jewel!

@lalaniij

Lalanii Wilson-Jones

TREAVION DAVENPORT

Hailing from the Motor City, Treavion, also known as "Trea," is a sought-after storyteller, ghostwriter, film, and TV producer. When she isn't creating content and bringing characters to life on pages, stages, and screens, she's running her highly lauded PR and strategic branding firm, Trea Day Management & Publicity. Based in Southern California, Trea enjoys adding stamps to her passport, adventures with her large family, and exotic cuisine. Her deepest passion is helping identify, refine, and make heard the voices of those who might otherwise be silenced.

@treadavenport

Trea Denise Davenport

@sugarmamabook

www.ultimatesugarmama.com